MW00878908

ELEVATION

SAMANTHA CONNOR

Cover designed by Kylie Knapp

Samantha Connor
Visit my website at www.elevationnovel.com

Printed in the United States of America

ISBN-13 9781717972378

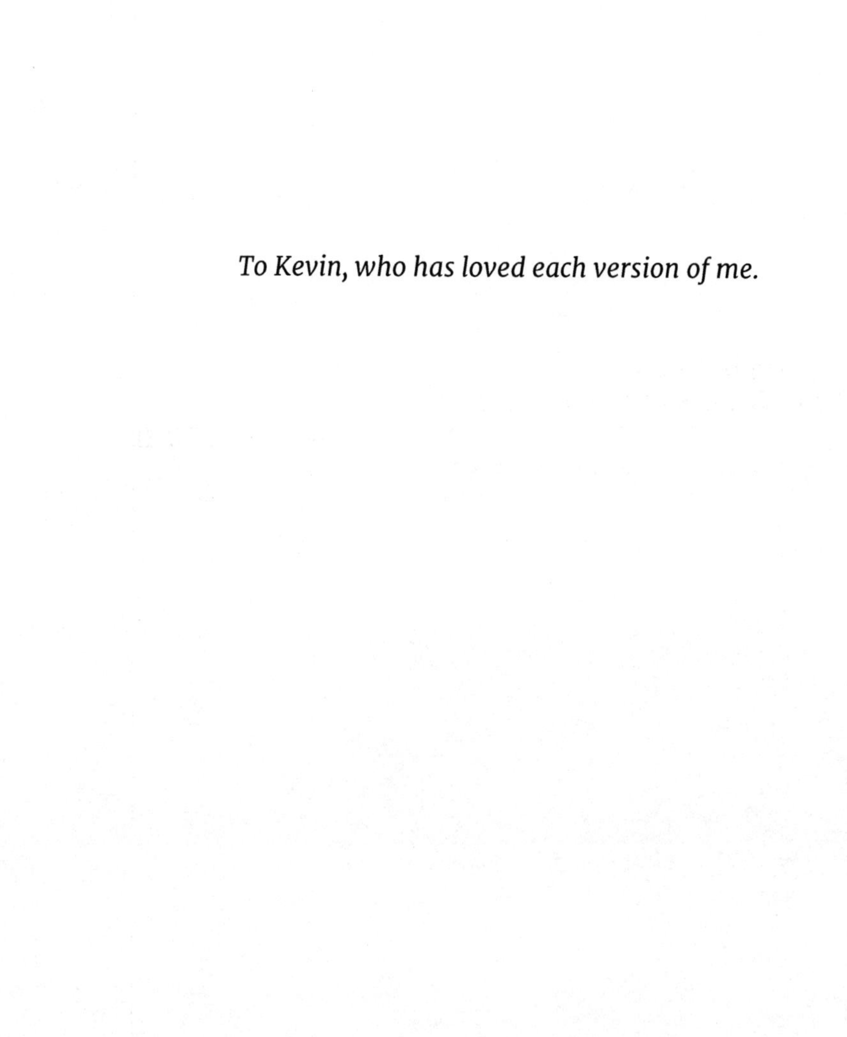

To Kevin, who has loved each version of me.

No one is you
and that is your power

—DAVE GROHL

CONTENTS

1 YEAR 28 (2016)

KENDALL

Golden beet and arugula niçoise salad topped with sashimi tuna. Imperial crab risotto infused with truffle oil. Sweet potato bacon latke in a maple béarnaise sauce.

The lighting's wrong in that last one. The digital photo didn't capture the golden-orange, glistening potato pillows in their full glory like I'd hoped. Amateur Instagram foodies might manipulate the image with filters before posting to make the photo more visually appealing, but I'm a purest. The food should speak for itself without false elements. It should be good enough in the first place, or in this case, the sixteenth. My idol, Susan Wilder, says that the true beauty of the culinary arts is in the subtleties of a well-planned and well-presented menu and should begin with perfection in all elements of one's meal. So the first fifteen latkes ended up in the bottom of my impeccably clean trash can.

As I sit here putting the final touches on my pre-Thanksgiving-feast blog several months early (topic: *The American History of the Cranberry*), I realize I still have a lot left to finish preparing for tomorrow. And it's nearly midnight. In a mild panic after this discovery, I rush around the apartment, throwing together some ingredients for an apple spice loaf for tomorrow's blog (*Quick Breads for a Slow Morning*), clean the dishes, straighten up my tiny kitchen, and head to the closet to pick out and iron my clothes for the next morning. As I pass by my computer screen, I hear a small 'ping' indicating a new comment on yesterday's post. When I hear this noise, my whole world stops. I'm simultaneously elated and afraid of the unknown text waiting beyond my log-in. My shirt could be on fire, and I would check the words on the small lit screen before I stop, drop and roll. I page down and I'm confronted by the words—

YOUR LIFE IS EMPTY.

I let my breath out, which I realize I've been holding. Against my better judgment, I quickly keep scanning through the post.

...like the boxed cake mix you made that coconut cake with...
...full of lies...
...you plagiarize recipes...

I freeze. My worst nightmare has come to fruition. I'm being trolled. I stare back at those first four words and the approximate hundred that follow them, each exploding with hatred and disgust at who they think I am and what my blog represents. This is not the first time I've gotten negative feedback on posts but it is definitely the most detailed and feels the most personal. After re-reading the painful essay that puts my biggest fears into words, I'm nauseous and shaking. But I'm not going to just sit back and let this troll destroy all of my hard work and all of my success with a late-night rant. So I sit down at the keyboard and begin typing a response into the void. Then I remember Susan Wilder's most recent email with her advice on this topic. When you become a public success, you are going to have people who want to put you down. Don't show them you're vulnerable to their insults. Don't engage. They are beneath you. I take a deep breath, holding down the backspace key until my words are once again white space in the Reply field. Then I scroll back up through the previous comments.

Loved this recipe! U R Awesome!

> *Thank you for such an awesome post. I am totes jealous of your life :)*
>
> *Can't wait to try. Check out my post too @ 5minmenu.com*

There are hundreds of these, and most of them are from people I don't even know. People that love my blog and took the time to tell me. And they are the people that matter. Not this bottom-feeder. I stand from the laptop and look out my tiny window to the lights of the city that never sleeps. From the tenth floor, I can see people walking past each other quickly. New Yorkers don't walk without purpose, and it's calming to me to know that they are exactly where they are supposed to be. The golden and white lights intermingle with small flashes of green and red, and you can see everything in clear detail even this late in the night, down to the cracks in the sidewalk.

> *EMPTY.*
> *How could my life be empty?*

I am living in this highly-sought-after, four-hundred square foot apartment, in New York City. I have a closet full of designer clothes that I bought with my hard-earned money, and I have thousands of followers of my blog who support me. I am up here sitting literally on top of the world. So since Manhattan is only twenty-one feet above sea level I decide to think of this troll as a swamp dweller. And she needs to crawl back in her hole where she came from. I have places to be and ceilings to break. So I hit *Remove post* without hesitation.

There is a celebratory beep from the oven, and the smells of cloves and cinnamon wafts through the small space around me. I grab my camera from the desk and a potholder from the wall over the sink. I open the oven, and as the golden light kicks on, it reveals an oddly shaped mass that does not at all resemble a loaf. It's more like a soggy pancake. In a fit of rage, I throw the whole pan into the sink, apple spice pancake and all, and the metal Bundt pan sounds like a loud gong when it hits the sink bottom. I stare at the steam coming off of the hot steel and feel my confidence evaporating with it. This was supposed to be an easy sell and be a top pin on Pinterest by tomorrow, and now I have to start over. How the hell am I going to become a major influencer when I can't even come up with a simple, unleavened bread recipe? Or take a decent picture of a fucking orange latke?

Out of desperation I pull the pancake-loaf out of the pan, burning my fingers in the process, and plop it on one of my best white porcelain cake stands. I beat cream cheese, sugar, and cream into submission with my hand mixer and shovel it onto the soggy pancake, and then I wrap it into a giant burrito like a buche de noel. I take a million pictures from every angle possible and write an upbeat post about how autumn is coming in New York and apple is the new pumpkin. I hit *Enter*, and a wave of satisfaction moves through me. I am Kendall Gibbons, and tomorrow is the culmination of all my hard work and perseverance. It's the beginning of my new life.

Tomorrow is not really an interview per se, but one of the most important networking opportunities of my entire career. Susan Wilder is one of the most well-known figures in the self-made food blogging industry. She practically invented avocado toast. She's a genius.

With this thought, I stand facing my three-tiered closet and I'm paralyzed by indecision, a feeling I haven't really experienced since before I decided to take the plunge into the food blog world several years ago. But tomorrow I don't have the option to be anything less than perfect. After flipping through every single hanger twice, I try on the black suit and then the collared shirt, and then the sweater, but I hate them all. And all of my outfit changes take three times longer than usual because I am compulsively ironing each piece of clothing after taking it off my body.

It is now 12:36, and I have to be awake in approximately six hours for the most important interaction of my adult life. My laptop screen-saver flickers on, shining brightly in the dimly lit apartment and taunting me. On it, a photo of Susan Wilder smiles with ease, a mixing bowl and whisk in hand and a Hermes scarf hugging her impeccably tan and smooth face.

Let's get together and toss around ideas, she said in her email. *How's 8:30 on Monday?*

When she's typing this, I imagine she is simultaneously whipping meringue for the top of a scratch-made lemon custard tart and kissing her perfect husband and children goodnight while her homemade Christmas ornaments dry on the kitchen table. (The ornaments are, of course, all custom monogrammed by hand and represent each recipient's zodiac sign.) Her words bounce around in my head as I wash and dry my short, blond hair a second time. Then I straighten it into submission, making sure my side-swept bangs lay correctly over my too-large forehead. I decide if I prop my head up with two large pillows I can ensure that I won't roll over and pancake them in my sleep. I turn out the lights and try to tell myself that my hard work is paying off. That things are happening. And then I tell my mind to shut up. Again. And Again.

The red glow of the alarm clock is now the only light illuminating my tiny studio apartment. It shines *2:10 AM*, which means I am officially desperate for anything to stop the never-ending flow of thoughts in my mind. I open my nightstand and a half-empty bottle of Ambien beckons to me. Then, I begin to rationalize the decision that my anxious mind has already made—if I only take a half a pill, I will wake up refreshed and one step closer the Kendall I always dreamed I would be. A stunning Internet sensation with her own fascinating and well-sponsored blog. I swallow half a pill, lay my head back down gently on my pillows, and chant my mantra to myself until a dreamless Ambien haze takes over my body: I am in control. I am in control. I am in control. Finally, my endless thoughts are overtaken by pharmaceutical sleep, empty and brief.

2

KENDALL

It takes me a moment to recognize that I'm still in my bed, and that the screeching noise next to my head is my alarm clock. Smacking it, I note the time and after recalling the importance of this morning, I realize I overslept by an hour. I have no time to shower and still get over to Wilder's office in time.

I stumble out of bed and around the apartment, grabbing my clothes, smoothing out the back of my blond bob, and brushing some powder over my tired face. I glance in the mirror for a brief once-over, and I shudder at the mess of a woman staring back at me. But tardiness is not an option, especially if I want any kind of a shot at earning her endorsement. With no time for my normal subway route, I flag down a cab, bark the address to the driver, and we are off.

After a fruitless attempt at makeup application during the ride over, I run out of the cab and into the impressively large lobby of one of the tallest buildings in the city. The floor is marble and the trim gold, with large, polished pillars and several benches where no one actually stops to sit.

The only sound comes from a television behind an empty security desk that's playing an old episode of *The Nanny* in Spanish. I can tell because even in dubbed Spanish, the Fran Drescher-esque voice mocks me with her signature cackle as I nearly eat marble tripping on my own feet on my way to the front desk. The security guard must be on break, and I don't have time to wait, so I rush over to the elevator and pound the open button, praying that I don't need an access badge for the fifteenth floor. I check my hair and outfit in my reflection of the elevator door and again feel a rush of discouragement and disgust wash over me. I'm overall very average. My height is short to average, my hair is dull and washed out from all the bleach, and there is just nothing spectacular about me. I will never be good enough for Susan Wilder. I took the easy way out by taking a sleeping pill, and now I'm so groggy and disheveled that I'm going to fail before I even begin.

When the elevator doors open, the eery silence of the interior is unnerving. This is one of the busiest areas of the city, and the building still seems completely empty. I step inside the gilded gold box, turn around, and the doors slowly come together in front of me. I suddenly feel claustrophobic, and my mind, still possibly clouded by the half an Ambien, is muddled with confusion and the beginnings of panic—*Is it Saturday? Did you sleep for six days? Did you miss the meeting? Where is the elevator music*?

Mid-thought, there's a deafening thump and I'm jolted by a violent shift that nearly knocks me to the floor. I brace myself with my arm on the elevator wall and manage to shift my legs back into a crouched but upright position. The lights flicker around me, and I can't recall pushing an elevator button. I look towards the control buttons and they are all still unlit. With a very loud 'ding' the 15 is spontaneously illuminated. My throat feels like it's closing in on itself. The interior elevator lights flicker again, and the doors slowly begin to open to what I assume is the fifteenth floor. My mind is at first swirling with confusion and terror, but as I slowly ease my body into standing position and pass through the elevator door, I can't seem to recall where Susan Wilder's office is anymore.

3
YEAR 15

KENDALL

The bright fluorescent lighting of the fifteenth-floor lobby hits my eyes immediately, and I'm forced to pause for a moment to let them adjust to the change. Still feeling a bit hazy, I approach a front desk. The young woman behind the desk doesn't look up at me, but I am acutely aware of her familiarity.

Have I met her before?

The young receptionist, who is completely ignoring my presence, is dressed in a confusing combination of crocheted halter top and tight white capri pants. She twirls a long blonde curl around her finger and chews gum loudly while flipping through a magazine. It would be a drastic understatement to say that the decor of the fifteenth-floor lobby is unimpressive. Rather it is non-existent. There are horrible neon lights scattered throughout a tiled ceiling, dirty green linoleum floors, and random metal filing cabinets stacked in no particular order. The large desk in front of me is littered with papers and file folders, with a lack of organization that is down-right appalling. The admin still does not look up but continues flipping pages and chomping on her gum at an alarmingly rapid pace.

I hear myself say, "Hi, I'm Kendall Gibbons. I have an appointment with Susan Wilder."

She looks up at me very briefly with a scowl and returns to her magazine.

"Excuse me," I enunciate more, clearing my throat and internally worrying that I might still be under the influence of the sleeping pill, "I'm sorry if I wasn't clear, but—"

"Look, I don't know what you're talking about Kendall, but Miss Peterson is on the phone right now. Just sit down and she'll come get you when she's done."

She motions over to a tattered orange tweed couch that looks like it hasn't been cleaned in the better part of a decade.

"I'm not sure if you heard me corr—" my voice trails off as I realize that she is ignoring me. Her fingers are hunting and pecking on a desktop computer that looks like it's even older than the sofa. A dial-up modem sounds loudly over her typing, and she pauses, checking her nails and waiting for the connection. I start to back away from the desk in fear, and I am stopped by a voice.

"Kendall," a woman to my left interrupts, "I just got off the phone with your mother. C'mon back."

My mother?

My palms start sweating and my whole body feels like it's on fire. Not only are this office and the admin oddly recognizable, but so is the woman called Miss Peterson. *She was my high school guidance counselor.*

Miss Peterson is a large woman with a puff of brown hair that always manages to rest on her head like a helmet. She has reading glasses that look like they might fall off the tip of her nose at any moment. Her face is round, her features small and doll-like in the middle of it, and she's flushed from exertion as I remember her to be one of those people who is constantly overwhelmed by life.

She quickly and exhaustingly takes a seat behind her desk and looks at me with a combination of pity and concern, "So let's talk about what happened today in Mr. Feldman's class."

My heart pounds in my ears, muffling her words. I have a sensation that my mind is separating from my body—and suddenly this adult-size cabbage patch kid appears to be fifty yards away from me instead of fifty inches. I have no idea what's happening to me, or what to say to her, so I look down at my hands. There are little white daisies painted on my ring fingers, and my hands rest atop my thighs, which are covered in a short jean skirt with a frayed hem. I rub my sweaty palms on the skirt and realize that I'm missing something. Specifically, the skin on my knee is missing a large scar that I got in college when I fell running for a train. My breathing becomes more shallow and rapid and I'm starting to sweat all over. I fear I may pass out.

This has to be a dream. Or a nightmare.

Miss Peterson is still staring at me, waiting for a response.

"I—I'm not sure what you mean?"

"Kendall, you are in a safe place now. We can talk about your preferences openly here."

And then the memory of this day comes rushing back to me vividly, like most traumatic experiences do.

—

I spent all week preparing for the mid-semester monologue in Mr. Feldman's class, making sure I memorized the passage so that I wouldn't pass out or throw up when it came time to get up in front of everyone. He graded on accuracy of memorization of the iambic pentameter with bonus points for dramatic delivery. So earlier that morning in the locker room, when I was changing after a particularly brutal gym class, I was going over and over the lines in my head. I was so absorbed in remembering the words, that had no idea I was staring at Kim Mason's breasts the entire time. By the time of the monologue, unbeknownst to me, the entire sophomore class apparently did. I didn't even get through the first two lines before the 'dike' coughs began. My first reaction was to pretend I didn't hear the perpetrators, but my emotions got the best of me, and my face turned scarlet and then white. But anything less than one-hundred percent has always been unacceptable for Kendall Gibbons, so I continued my assignment as the tears began to well up in my eyes. I finished the last verse and instinctively ran for the closest exit before my sobs became audible to my classmates.

—

"Being a homosexual is nothing to be ashamed of," Miss Peterson continued, "I just don't want this to affect your academic performance, and, you know, make you draw attention to yourself in negative ways."

I have not thought about this day in at least ten years. I think my fifteen-year-old reaction was naturally one of shame and denial, and Miss Peterson's was one of patronizingly simple conclusions and sugarcoated discrimination.

"I think it's just confusing to the rest of us, who aren't, you know, like you," she says, while looking over my shoulder at an unspecified spot on the wall behind me.

She squeezes a tissue into a tiny wad in her hand, which I stare at in disbelief. I can't believe I'm having a dream about this woman, sitting there nervously behind her over-sized metal desk that's covered in coffee rings and cat figurines.

But my mind does not respond like my fifteen-year-old mind might have all those years ago. I am overwhelmed with anger, rather than juvenile embarrassment. I can't believe that this authority figure would single someone out as disruptive and make them feel abnormal and wrong for their sexual orientation, even if that orientation was misinterpreted on her part. "I thought you of all people would understand, Miss Peterson, but it seems like I thought too highly of you. Looks like you're a bigot too, but you're even worse than a bunch of small-minded fifteen and sixteen-year-olds because your brain is done developing. The neuropathways are set. So I guess there's no hope for you, and you'll be sitting here looking down on high schoolers while they escape this place and become lawyers, doctors, and executives and decide whether your precious school budget gets cut. Looks like your pathetic fate is actually in those idiots' hands. Might as well just sit here and wait for your pitiful tenure while you get fatter by the minute eating government-approved chicken nuggets and French fries."

4

MIKE

I'm sitting here drumming my fingers on the dashboard along with the Red Hot Chili Peppers and staring at the clock. I look around the parking lot and when I look back, not even a minute has passed since he walked into the store.

"C'mon, dude—" I mutter under my breath.

Gavin comes running out of the gas station with a wide grin and jumps into the passenger seat. I don't put the car into gear yet. I just stare at Gavin, expressionless and waiting. "So did you get it?"

"Get what?" Gavin smiles.

I punch him in the shoulder.

"Ow! Freaking chode! That's my shooting arm!" he exclaims, rubbing the point of impact.

"I swear to God, if you didn't get it—"

"Just chill out, here—" he tosses a small box over my lap, and it falls between the door and the driver's seat.

I pick it up and take a deep breath, "Let's go see if my life is over." I shove the pregnancy test in my cargo pants pocket and reverse out of the parking spot.

After several minutes of driving through the tree-lined streets of Sunnyvale, the music blaring out of my cracked window, Gavin shouts to be heard over the music, "Look, man, it could be okay. Your mom and dad might be stoked to know they'll be grandparents— might be their only chance. With your sister being a lesbian and all."

I make a sharp turn into his cracked concrete driveway and slam the brakes, causing his head to come within an inch of the dashboard and then snap back into the headrest.

"Get out of my fucking car, dude," I say, trying to stifle a smile, as Gavin falls out of the car laughing. "Thank you for the pee stick and for generally being more of an asshole than me."

Gavin tips an invisible hat towards me and then calls through the cracked window, "Hey, Kendall's hot. I'd pay good money to watch that!"

"Gavin, I will run you over if you don't shut the fuck up. Bye." I drive away and turn up the music.

I make a right turn, and then another right turn, and then another right turn, and pull over on the side of a small neighborhood road. I put the car in park and let my head fall against the top of the steering wheel.

5

KENDALL

In most dreams, the world can almost instantly transform around you, but it feels nearly effortless. And then suspension of disbelief keeps you moving in whatever direction your subconscious chooses. Leonardo DiCaprio taught me that.

This particular dream seems to be an exception to that. It is long and monotonous, and I have to walk everywhere to get where I want to go. Also, I don't seem to have any control over anyone else in the dream. And it's super boring. So when the final bell rings in my last period, I begin the long walk to my parents' house, hopeful that eventually I'll wake up in my bed and get ready for my meeting with Susan Wilder.

It's a warm and sunny September day in northern California. I can feel the warmth of the sun against the top of my head, and the dry, soft breeze through my long hair. I walk the two miles very slowly, thinking I may have been too harsh on Miss Peterson. My leg itches, so I stop to scratch it and the scab on my shin comes open, small beads of blood forming in its place. I wipe it off and leave a red smudge across my olive skin. A car full of teenage boys drives by me and honks and yells something I can't really understand. But I know it's not flattering.

Definitely a nightmare. A dull, super detailed nightmare.

I walk through the front door and the familiar smell of my childhood home greets me. The smell is inexplicable, kind of like the inside of an old wooden dresser. My house is small and dim, with very few windows on the first floor. The living room is off to the right of the foyer where I am standing—my dad's hideous gray recliner empty in the corner. The stairs are directly in front of me, with worn tan carpet lining them, and horrible elementary school photos of my brother and me all along the walls.

I try to consider what I would've done next, thirteen years ago. I'd probably have called my best friend Courtney from my bedroom to discuss the latest *Real World* episode, and then I would've spent an unreasonable amount of time reassuring her about her endless saga of insecurities, most notably her very large stature. Her nickname in high school was Sasquatch because she towered over almost everyone by at least six inches.

As I turn the corner from the foyer to the kitchen, which is a step up in our split-level home, my mom is sitting on a kitchen bar stool with her arms crossed and her keys in her hands. I jump backwards, nearly falling back down the step.

"I'm late for choir practice," she states, worriedly. We lock eyes, and I clutch my chest. She stares back at me, her expression unclear.

"You better hurry then—God's probably pissed," I say without thinking.

She makes a face that is part disgust and part disappointment. "Kendall, you know I can't just ignore a phone call like that from your guidance counselor," she pauses, "your father and I are very concerned about—your—choices..."

"Oh, God, Mom! I'm not a lesbian!" This part is the same, and I'm as pissed as I was that Friday back in 2003, "We've been through this over and over again. It was a mistake, a rumor. I like boys. I will date one eventually and you'll want me to marry him and I'll disappoint you and choose my career!"

My mom stands and looks at me, befuddled. Her tone is now quieter and more concerned, "Kendall, we have never discussed this before. What is going on with you? How could you get yourself suspended? And where is your brother? Did you walk all the way home?"

Shit- Mike. I used to ride home with Mike.

"You can forget about sleeping over at Courtney's this weekend. You are grounded."

"Grounded?"

"You cannot speak to me or Miss Peterson like those people on those trashy TV shows you are always watching. I am your mother. And you need some time to reevaluate your priorities. No TV, and no sleepovers."

I'm trying to remember how this played out in reality, but I can't recall being grounded. Of course I also didn't verbally assault an authority figure back then. Mostly I remember realizing for the first time that my mom didn't have all the answers. It was the first time she truly let me down. Instead of listening and comforting me, as a vulnerable misunderstood teenager, she made it her mission to fix me. In her eyes, I was a problem that could be solved with enough discipline and Bible verses.

As a watch her lecture me, her words are just rolling around in the room, failing to land on anything. I can't really focus on what she's saying, because I am studying the details of her face. Thirteen years ago, my mom was still relatively young, and the liveliness shows on her face. Like mine, her eyes are green, but her hair is a lighter, whitish blonde, pulled back with a butterfly clip at the bottom of her head. She could be pretty if she put in a little more effort. But instead she just looks resigned to her life of church, work, teenagers, and housework. It sounds heartless, but I never wanted to be like her. And the more she pushed me to be what she wanted me to be, the more I ran away. So I stopped coming home, first on college breaks, and then even on major holidays. It was easier for everyone that way.

My mom finally leaves for church, and I hear the garage door close. I listen as her car engine moves down the street until it's silent again.

I go up to my old bedroom and it's exactly how I remember it. I reach out and run my fingers over the glossy photos pinned to my bulletin board—

> *Courtney and I at the state fair last year, looking unimpressed.*
>
> *Mike giving me the middle finger (an image strategically covered by four Titanic movie stubs).*
>
> *Me holding my rabbit when I was about twelve years old. A rabbit who later escaped into the wild Californian suburban streets, never to be seen again.*

I plop down on the bed and as it springs back up, I can feel the weight of the room around me. I sit very still and stare straight ahead at the wall, going over the past few hours in my head.

After a few minutes of numb reflection, I stand up with a sudden sense of urgency and begin flicking the tiny metal piece of my elastic hair band against my wrist, over and over again. My skin stings and begins to turn light pink on the area of impact. Then I begin smacking my face, lightly at first, then repeatedly, and harder each time.

"Okay! Wake up!" I yell audibly. I run to the bathroom sink and splash my face with water. I look up, and into the mirror and staring back at me is a red-cheeked, partially soaked fifteen-year-old face.

Before I can think of my next move, I hear a car door slam and the front door open and shut. Loud footsteps jogging up the stairs.

Mike.

I run out of the bathroom and come face-to-face with my brother in the hallway. His hair is a shaggy mess on his head, and he's wearing his standard seventeen-year-old uniform of Mexican poncho and cargo pants, complete with tattered Vans. In his clutched right fist he's holding his usual skater hat. His eyes are not their typically lively bright blue, and I notice there are dark circles under them. He looks at me and I look back at him.

"Why are you wet?"

"Mike, I...I need...to talk to you. Now."

This is not something I would normally say to my brother. Typically we wouldn't even interact after school, and if we did it was to argue about something insignificant. Then I would storm away and pout and he would drive off to hang out with Gavin or Celeste.

"I really have to be somewhere," he says, coldly, staring over my shoulder.

"Please, Mike. I don't know what else to do."

He sighs and looks at his pocket. He walks into his room and leaves the door open for me to follow.

Mike starts riffling through the stacks of crap on his desk, looking for something underneath a layer of papers, folders and magazines.

"What's with you?" I ask, standing awkwardly in the middle of his room. I was never in here very much, "Mike, can you stop for a second? I need you to—"

"What? I don't—" he rummages around some more, finally stopping to look at me.

"—Hit me," I stare blankly back into his eyes.

"What?"

"Hit me in the face. Please."

"Alright, what the hell is going on? Did you find my weed or something?"

"Mike. I'm serious. I need you to hit me."

"Kendall, you're high. Let's just go get some Cheetos, and I'll put a movie on, and—"

"I'm not high! I'm twenty-eight years old and I need to get back to my life!"

"Twenty-eight years old? Alright, Kendall, where's my bowl? We need to get rid of the evidence before Mom and Dad—"

I grab his shoulders and shove my face inches from his, "Look at my eyes! I'm not stoned! You have to help me!"

He looks at my eyes very carefully and sits me down on his bed, calmly taking a seat on his desk chair across the room from me. After smoothing his hair back and replacing his hat backwards on his head, he looks over at me, mildly annoyed and a bit distracted, but at least he's looking at me to explain.

"Mike, you have to believe me. I thought I was dreaming—but then I had an itch and I bled and every detail of this house is so vivid and real and it's been so long—that I can't be—I think it's really...it's just that I'm not fifteen. I am twenty-eight years old. I woke up this morning as a twenty-eight-year-old and I went into this elevator and when I got out I was in the guidance counselor's office at our old high school. And I look like this."

There is a long pause of silence. "Did you play with one of those Zoltar machines last night or something? You were Tom Hanks before, weren't you?" He laughs at his own joke.

"I'm not joking, Mike."

"Look, I don't have time for this right now, I have to take care of something important."

He stands back up, patting his pockets to confirm their contents, and pulls out his car keys. He moves towards the door with a nervous energy that reminds me of myself last night. It's much more subtle, but it's there. My teenage brother didn't take many things seriously nor did he describe anything as important.

Rising from the bed, I take a chance, "Fine. I'm coming with you then."

He looks at me briefly, a heaviness in his light blue eyes. He opens his mouth like he wants to retort, but then he just turns around, opens the door and doesn't tell me not to follow him. I stay a step behind him as we walk quickly down the stairs, out the door, through the front yard, and up to his beat-up Camry. He ignores me, sliding into the driver's seat and I make a split-second decision to slide quietly and unassumingly into the back seat.

6

MIKE

Despite my outward appearance as a slacker-stoner type, I'm actually pretty intelligent. And good at math. So when I added up the weeks in my head, I realized there was no way it could have been me. I spent all of June and July training for lacrosse—my one shot at a college scholarship—and Celeste spent June and July pissed off at me. We fought for two months straight, and there was no silver-lining of makeup sex.

I pull the car up in front of Celeste's parents' house and cut the engine. I glance at my sister in the rear-view mirror and she's looking out the window, chewing her fingernails off in the back seat.

"Stay here."

I get out of the car and walk up the uneven brick path to the side entrance of the house. I had to get here before five because her parents will be making their way back from work and that would complicate things.

But, unexpectedly, the house is empty, and Celeste's car is not in the garage. In a moment of rage, I almost kick the door in, but thankfully I quickly talk myself out of this decision. Instead, I grab the spare key that I know is hidden under their mat and make my way through the kitchen and up the stairs to her bedroom. After checking a few drawers, I find a purple marker in her desk, pull out the $9.99 receipt for the pregnancy test, and use my gum to stick it to her mirror, right next to our Junior prom photo. I circle the name of the purchase for emphasis and write "We are fucking done. – Mike" carefully beneath it, so as not to obscure the type.

I take my time leaving, dropping the unopened pregnancy test on the kitchen counter, and grab a bottle of Mr. Donaldson's red wine from the rack nearby, as a final fuck-you to the whole family.

When fresh air hits my face, I instantly feel relief. I walk to the car slowly and drive off silently with Kendall in the back.

KENDALL

I don't say a word because I know he'll kick me out of the car if I annoy him. But the silence between us is killing me—I want to ask him what the hell he was doing and why he returned from Celeste's house with a bottle of wine. Then I want to demand that he take me to an airport so I can get on a plane back to New York immediately. Looking down at my knobby knees, I contain my urge to shout all of these demands at him from the back seat. I remind myself that I look fifteen—a young fifteen. I don't have the money to get anywhere and I probably couldn't even get through security without some kind of parental consent. Not to mention, my older brother hates my guts and would rather leave me on the side of the road then offer me any kind of assistance. I decide my best approach is to disappear for now, making him forget that I'm back here, and hope that I can come up with a plan before we have to go back to my parents' house.

We drive for five to ten minutes and end up outside of Gavin's house. Gavin is Mike's best friend since basically birth, and so by default I grew up seeing him nearly every day, first following him and Mike around trying to be like them, and then later competing with him for Mike's attention. A battle I always lost. Naturally I knew a great deal about him, at least up until our adolescence when our gender and age canyoned any of our mutual interests. I knew he loved boxed macaroni and cheese, snowboarding, and doing idiotic things like tying a jump-rope to the tree in our front yard to try to Tarzan-swing over the road. Gavin was effortlessly likable, and I was the opposite. When I made friends, it was often by default. Take Courtney for instance. My only real childhood friend was assigned to sit next to me on the bus when we were both granted the honored designation of Safety Patrol in the fall of fifth grade. Donning our neon orange belts and our bus numbers, we took turns alerting the less-conscientious first through fifth graders on when they could board and exit the bus. We took our job very seriously and so we instantly had a mutual understanding, which finally solidified itself with our discovery of 'NSYNC. Despite my introverted shortcomings as a conversationalist, Courtney began calling me nightly to talk about JC's hair. She drew me in with her dramatic exaggerations and overenthusiastic girlishness, putting me in makeup for the first time and teaching me to shave my legs even though I was technically two months her senior. Suddenly I didn't care about my brother and his goofy friend. Courtney and I would spend weekends gossiping and making up stories about people at school that we would act out in my room. I started writing them down in a composition book and soon I was making up new characters that we could become together. And Courtney loved it. I think both of us longed for an escape from the trials and tribulations of middle school. But as the years passed, we discovered boys and shopping, growing up and out of our childish games. We then spent most waking hours pleading with our mothers to drop us off at the mall, and eventually moved our pleading onto Mike, who was less than subtle regarding his feelings on the matter.

"Fuck off—I'm not taking you anywhere."

When I was around sixteen, my brother moved to Boulder for a lacrosse scholarship disguised as a college education and his sidekick Gavin followed.

Mike honks the horn and Gavin rambles out of the house, plopping into the passenger seat. He turns to put his bag behind his seat, and jumps a little, not expecting me to be there.

"Holy shit! Kendall!"

Gavin grins at me. He looks at Mike who is sullen and serious, his smile fading a bit, and back at me. I manage a small smile back.

"Are you coming to Greg's party with us?"

"Change of plans, Gav," Mike says as he drives off quickly, heading towards the main road.

Most people would question him, perhaps to find out a motivating factor for the deviation, or why I'm uncharacteristically present in the back seat, but Gavin does not worry about such minor details. As long as I've known him, he's been absolutely undeterred by change. He just turns up the stereo, bobbing his head to the beat, and no one says a word, as Mike navigates us to an unknown destination.

7

KENDALL

We pull into a quiet neighborhood street, not far from my parents' house, and then turn down another street that dead ends at the woods. Mike and Gavin both get out of the car and walk shoulder-to-shoulder, moving telepathically, Mike with the wine in his left hand and Gavin with his bag over his right. I follow silently.

We enter the thick woods and cross over a small stream, Mike and Gavin hopping from bank to bank easily. I try to follow suit, and stumble over a tree branch, nearly falling into the shallow water. Gavin grabs under my arm and helps me steady myself. I feel a shock go through my torso, and I pull my arm back, "Thanks. I got it."

Gavin just shakes his head, smiling, and catches up with Mike, who is making his way up a hill ahead of us. There is no real path, but Gavin and Mike both seem to know what trees to zig-zag between, and I follow them as closely as I can. The trees start to clear and in the grass-covered clearing, there are a few dirty, beat-up lawn chairs set up in a semi-circle in front of us, at the top of the hill. Glancing around in the dim light of dusk, I realize the hill is actually the very top of a train tunnel, with tracks exiting on either side.

I always knew this place existed, occasionally overhearing laughter and conversations about getting hammered and falling down the hill but was never allowed to know the exact location.

Gavin drops his bag and takes a seat on one of the old lawn chairs, and Mike sits on a larger one next to him. He pulls out a small pocket knife and starts silently cutting the foil off of the top of the stolen wine bottle, and then starts digging at the cork, chipping away at it slowly. Gavin grabs his bag, and pulls out two shitty light beers, handing one to Mike. Still, no one speaks. Mike puts the beer can in his cargo pocket and continues to chip away at the cork. Gavin pulls out a small stereo from his bag and puts in a cassette tape. I have to stifle a chuckle because I haven't seen a tape in well over ten years. He presses play and Eddie Vedder emotes from the speakers, strumming his way back to heaven. Since there are still no words between us, it's clear that this is a sacred place, and so I try to disappear.

After chugging three beers each, Mike has finally gotten almost all of the cork out of the bottle, though some of it is suspended in the wine below. He takes a big swig anyway and offers me the bottle. I accept it, gladly, and take a huge swig. Gavin laughs.

"Whoa whoa whoa, Ken, you're already high. Don't need you drunk too," my brother says sternly.

I take another sip and lean back, closing my eyes and transporting myself back to my favorite cafe in the Village. I speak without thinking, "This Merlot is delicious. It has subtle notes of juniper berries, stone fruit, and," I sniff the top of the bottle, "a hint of cocoa."

"What *the fuck* are you talking about?"

I open my eyes and Mike and Gavin are both staring at me. Gavin looks at Mike, and Mike looks at me, adding, "Oh yeah, she's pretending to be twenty-eight today."

Gavin then looks over at me, and I adjust my posture so I'm sitting up perfectly straight on the edge of the lawn chair. Somehow I feel a slightly buzzed, warm feeling from the two sips of wine.

"Don't patronize me, asshole."

They both take a swig of their beers, laughing, and Mike throws his empty into a growing pile in front of him.

"I'll prove it to you."

"Oh, really?" he rolls his eyes.

Gavin stops the tape and fiddles with the radio dial, turning up the music ever so slightly, "I love this song, man."

They are both silent as Johnny Cash's *Hurt* plays over the radio. A DJ breaks the radio silence, "The Man in Black, looking down on us from rock 'n roll heaven with June by his side—" he pauses to let his audience recover, "—be sure to join us tomorrow night for our free concert downtown. Proceeds go to September Eleventh first responder families. Tons of bands, all night long. Goodbye all, I'm signing off. Johnny, Rest in Peace."

I think for a beat, marveling that nine-eleven is still such a fresh wound at this point in time. That time really does heal, or at least it numbs.

September of 2003, I hug my arms to my body, rubbing the goose bumps away. It's an unexpectedly cool fall evening.

And all of a sudden, a wave of memory crashes all around me. Remembering a key piece of information about this time and place of my young life, I'm suddenly brave.

"I'll prove it to you," I say as I approach Gavin, and quickly grab the beer box at his feet. I dump out the remaining beer cans into the grass and rip off a piece of cardboard. I dig in my purse for a pen and start furiously scribbling on the brown cardboard back of the beer box.

"I guess we have to drink the rest of this case, my friend," Gavin laughs, holding his beer out towards Mike in an air-toast.

I hold out the piece of beer box, now folded in two, "Gavin, you're the objective third party. Carry this with you until tomorrow night and show Mike at ten PM. And then you'll have to believe me."

"Believe what?" Gavin asks, not taking the cardboard.

"That this morning I woke up and I was twenty-eight years-old. And somehow I got out of an elevator and I'm fifteen...again."

Mike laughs at me, "Fine tell us about the future then. Tell us what happens to us in thirteen years."

"Am I a pro-lacrosse player? Or snowboarder?" Gavin asks sarcastically.

My tone is serious, "I don't know, Gavin. I stopped talking to you after I left high school."

"Oh, damn, Mike and I aren't even friends in the future? It must be some alternate universe, like *BiffCo* or something."

"Nice *Back to the Future* reference," Mike laughs.

"No—I don't see Mike at all either. Not even on holidays. I have no idea what you guys are doing."

They are both silent for a second, seemingly deep in thought.

"I bet I'm rich as shit, man!" Gavin throws an empty beer can at Mike who laughs and runs over to tackle Gavin.

They ignore me as they finish the last of the beers and go off to pee in the woods. I find my way back to the car in silence, clutching my cardboard note and the boys stumble after me, laughing and talking nonsense.

Mike hands me the keys, "You crash it, I kill you."

Gavin comes up from behind and puts his large arm over my shoulders. At six-foot-three, he's about a head taller than me and has that teenage boy too-skinny-for-his-body look. He has olive skin with a small amount of acne on his chin, and shaggy brown hair that falls in his eyes when he's not wearing a backwards baseball hat— a hat which hasn't been washed in a minimum of five years. He looks at me with his slightly drunken, but deep brown eyes, "Kendall, why don't you hang out with us more? You're really awesome. I mean, you're definitely way cooler than Mike."

I lock eyes with him and he gets a sort-of worried look on his face, dropping his arm to his side. He yells "Shotgun!" and his shit-eating grin is back in no time.

I pull the car into our driveway, and the boys tumble out of the car and into the side door of the garage. They immediately fall into place on either end of our living room sofa and turn on *Super Troopers*. Thankfully, our parents are already in bed, so there are no excuses or explanations needed. As I walk over to the kitchen to get a glass of water, I spot Gavin's bag on the kitchen floor by the door. I quickly unzip the back compartment and put the cardboard truth inside, zipping it up tightly.

8

MIKE

I wake up on the couch to the sound of a vacuum piercing through my skull. The light from the living room window feels like a punch to the face. After my eyes adjust, I look at the end of the couch, and Gavin is gone. I look up and Kendall is running the vacuum attachment over the arm of the couch, right next to my pillow.

"Do you seriously have to do that now?" I moan loudly over the vacuum.

"Yes. Tonight's mom's birthday party and she's out getting her nails done. We only have a little while to make this place look perfect."

I grab my hat from between the couch cushions and head up to my room to escape the noise.

I flop onto the bed and realize it's made for the first time in years. In my hungover haze, I notice the room is clean and smells—different. Kind of like lemonade.

I have to pee and my mouth feels like I've been sucking on a dirty penny all night, so I head to the bathroom relieve myself and get some water. The sink is a lot whiter than usual and hair-free. There's a candle lit in the corner, and there are no wet towels on the floor. My poncho is also nowhere to be found.

"Kendall!"

I stomp into her room and she's sitting on a chair throwing most of the contents into her desk into the trash can in front of her.

"Where the fuck is my poncho?"

"I burned it."

"Shut up and tell me where it is."

"No."

"Look, just because you think it's fun to act like you're twenty-eight doesn't give you the right to be a neat-freak bitch. I don't care what you're working on this time but leave me out of it."

"Mike, this isn't a game. I know I used to do those childish pretend plays all the time, but that ended a long time ago."

"What, like last week? Or when everyone called you a lesbian at school yesterday?"

"Fuck off, this has nothing to do with that! You can have your precious poncho back after you help me get back to my life."

"Suck it, Kendall. I'm going to practice, and when I get back, that poncho better be on my bed and it better not smell like fucking potpourri."

9

KENDALL

T*hink, Kendall. You need a better plan.*

My plan to convince Mike that I'm really twenty-eight has failed so far, leaving a solution still out of reach.

Even if I can get Mike to believe me, what is he even going to help me do?

I pace around my bedroom, scanning the walls, the floor, the furniture for inspiration. For anything. I head downstairs for the one thing that might be of use to me right now, and after moving some folders and boxes off of my dad's desk, I sign onto the dusty family desktop and wait an eternity for the modem to connect. If there's one thing I know how to do, it's research.

I start with several search engines that are irrelevant in 2016 and, as anticipated, get very few hits.

"Change to a different age" gets me cosmetic surgery offices and self-help books, "28 and then 15" gets me multiplication tables, "turned into younger self" gets me healthy-eating magazine articles and ads for special face lotions. After almost an hour of word-smithing, I'm not much closer to an answer than when I started my search, and I've rediscovered my limitations in the world before ubiquitous Wi-Fi and smart phones. Wikipedia is not at all reliable, with very few topics that have been confirmed, and other than a few articles about Stephen Hawking, the Internet sources on worm holes and time travel are limited in 2003. Partially as an internal joke, I decide to type "How does someone travel into the past?" into AskJeeves.com. I hit *Enter* and a number of weird science-nerd chat boards come up. Some things never change. There are a bunch of pseudonyms like *VaderHater81* and *DragonRider2616* talking about quantum physics and the light-sound barrier. While most of it is over my head, some is mildly interesting.

For instance, the grandfather paradox. The logical side of quantum physics says that time travelers could not, by nature, travel back in time in human form. The rationale, according to science, is that any effect they had on their past would invariably cause disruption to their future and this would cause them to cease to exist in the "present." My heart stops.

Does this mean I may have ceased to exist as a twenty-eight-year-old?

Reading on, the main disruption exists, in theory, if I were the actual creator of the time machine. So in other words if my past didn't happen exactly as it did, then I would not have been able to create a vessel to travel back in time in in the future. But I didn't create anything, or even want to travel back in time. I'm just here, and I was there.

My brain hurts from just considering this, and the cosmic implications are too much for me right now. Scrolling down the results page, I find a lighter and more creative avenue— synopses of several eighties and nineties movies involving time travel or personal transformation. Of these, the most popular are *Big*, *Back to the Future* trilogy, and *Bill and Ted's Excellent Adventure*.

Great.
So according to Hollywood, I am going to need:
A. A carnival game.
B. A discontinued pseudo-luxury car transformed into a time machine.
C. Keanu Reeves. And a phone booth.

Despite my growing frustration over the increasingly useless search results, I jot down notes from each source like I am prepping for one of my blogs. I scan over them, looking for any kind of pattern between theory, pop culture, and my unfortunate reality.

Connecting very existential dots, I decide to focus my energy on the least common denominator— the majority of the theoretical and fictitious time travelers had to have a vessel of some kind to transport them through a fold in time. A worm-hole, a black hole—they all have different terminology for it but essentially it is gap in time that allows the traveler to skip over dimensions and penetrate time as if they are outside of its rules. And the geeks on the message boards emphasize the dangers of an unprotected human hurtling through a worm hole. Apparently there is a great potential for a human to molecularly rearranged into cosmic pudding without some kind of structure to protect them from the energy that time travel requires.

So here's what I know about my situation: in a pharmaceutical haze, I got into an elevator. When I got out I was in my fifteen-year-old body. I still have my twenty-eight-year-old brain with all its damage and baggage and endless perfectionism, but my physical state and the physical world around it is almost exactly as it was in 2003. And that's all I can come up with. I was too busy worrying about my future to notice that my present world had transformed around me.

Maybe I can find the answer in what I do remember—I entered the elevator in 2016 and I exited in 2003.

This sparks an idea.

Maybe it wasn't when I got out but where I got in?

After writing out the details of what occurred that day, I come to the most logical conclusion in a situation that's lacking any kind of logic at all. That even though I'm not in Manhattan, there are skyscrapers and elevators that are just as tall in nearby San Jose. And I have access to a car. So, tonight, I'll convince my idiot brother to take me to a building with at least twenty-eight floors and see if there's some portal in the elevator that will get me back to my life. Worst comes to worst, I'll just jump off the roof if this doesn't work.

After several more minutes of fruitless searching on the amazingly slow Internet, the only option that I can seem to find, that might be realistically possible to get to as a fifteen-year-old, is my father's office building downtown. But I'll of course need a ride there, and a way to get into the elevator alone. Mike can provide a ride at least, because there's no way I can convince my dad in twenty-four hours that I have to go to work with him. After convincing Mike to drop me off I'll have to formulate a plan for when and how I can make the rest of the pieces fit together. In the meantime, my fate is riding on a piece of cardboard in the hands of a seventeen-year-old clown.

10

MIKE

Well, it's certainly going to be a shitastic Saturday night at the Gibbons household. My mom's having a dinner party for her birthday, which means a bunch of her choir friends and Dad's work people asking me over and over again where I'm going to college and what I'm gonna major in. Luckily Gavin's irresponsible uncle can be counted on for only one thing—getting so loaded that he doesn't notice when we steal his beer.

Gavin flings open my bedroom door and it thumps against the *Good Charlotte* poster behind it. He's wearing cutoff jean shorts that look like he borrowed them from my ex-girlfriend, a flannel shirt and a straw hat. And of course, his standard shit-eating grin. The party has arrived.

"What the hell are you wearing, man?"

"Late night party at Tasha's after her parents pass out. She said we can't come unless we dress up, and I'm trying to touch those boobies tonight!"

"Dress up like what? Freaking homos?"

"I don't know, it's like 'wild wild west' or some gay shit. But you can't argue my legs aren't incredible in these shorts," he poses with one leg straight and the other bent and flying out to the side.

"Tasha's a lucky woman."

"Damn straight, man," as he pops open his first beer, I hear the doorbell ring.

"Gimme two of those."

—

Three beers deep and I'm starting to feel brave about sneaking out tonight. To avoid suspicion, I have to at least walk downstairs and be seen around the party first and then get my sister to cover for us. Which may prove to be difficult with her recent onset of extra-bitchiness. I knock on the door of her room, Gavin close behind me. She opens it only a crack, and I poke my foot through the crack, pushing it open a little more.

"You guys smell like beer," she says as she grabs my elbow and pulls me through the door. Gavin practically falls through after me, and she closes the door quickly behind us. She sits us on the bed and gives us each a stick of gum and sprays us with a bottle of something that smells like clean laundry.

"Whoa, Ken—" I cough, "—what the hell? Stop it!"

"You can't go out there reeking of shitty beer and talk to Dad. He'll never let you take the car."

"Who says we're taking the car?"

"Look, I know you're sneaking out. And I'll help you get the keys if you promise to drop me off first."

"No way! Mom and Dad will definitely notice if we're all gone. We need you to cover for us—tell mom we had to go back to Gavin's to get—our sticks or something."

"Yea, for practice tomorrow," Gavin adds.

"Look, I'm getting out of here and you can either help me, or I'll tell Mom you took the car."

"Dammit, Ken," Mike pauses, grabbing the front of his hair in his fist and letting it go dramatically, "let's go downstairs. But you need to act freaking normal."

"You guys need to act sober!"

Gavin just starts giggling and in his uncontrollable laughter, he slips off the bed with a loud thud against my bedroom floor, "I love you Kendall. You're so freaking weird and I love it."

"Shut up Gavin!" we both turn towards him, yelling in unison.

11

KENDALL

After I convince Gavin to put on some pants and lose the ridiculous hat, the boys surprisingly hold it together for the duration of the time we are downstairs. So far my revised plan is working, and they haven't left without me yet. The first time around, I remember Mike was grounded for at least a month after my mom went up to check on him and he was nowhere to be found. And I was stuck at home with my parents all night waiting for the dynamic duo to stumble back into the house and get in trouble.

"So Kendall I hear you are quite the thespian."

I nearly spit my soda out all over my parents' friend Roger's baby blue polo shirt. His face is expectant, waiting for my response. I try to gather my composure but all that comes out of my mouth is, "huh?"

"Your mom said you love the theater—that you're something of an amateur playwright."

"Oh, um, yea I guess. My friend Courtney likes acting so I try to write stuff for her to, you know, act."

Roger nods, smiling, and then begins a five-minute diatribe about his experience in community theater. I smile and try to act interested, my mind drifting back to my childhood friend again. We spent so much time together creating these characters personalities before we even had an idea of our own. It strikes me that even back then my greatest goal was to pretend my way through life.

As Roger wraps up his story about his recent contemporary adaptation of *My Fair Lady*, out of the corner of my eye I catch Mike and Gavin heading back upstairs towards Mike's room. I check my watch, and excuse myself, walking quickly after them. Mike slams the door behind them and it clicks, locked.

I knock on the door loudly, in rapid succession, and use my best mom-voice, "Michael James!"

There's no response, and no sign of movement on the other side of the door. I slam my fists against it, holding them against the wood for a beat, and hanging my head. I search my mind for any trace of a memory—anything that might lead me in the direction of Mike. In the distance, I hear the very faint sound of a car trunk slamming.

Trying not to draw attention to myself, I run down the stairs low and on my toes, moving quietly out past the foyer and onto the front stoop just as Mike is pulling out of our driveway—Gavin in the front seat next to him.

I then make an impulsive and drastic decision.

I sprint out into the street to block their path, and Mike swerves to miss me and nails a telephone pole in front of my neighbor's yard. There's a deafening bang followed by a crunching sound, and through the smoke I can see that the pole now leans slightly towards the car. I run over to them.

"Kendall, what the fuck!?" Mike yells as he gets out of the car and grabs his head in a panic, "Oh God! Oh God! Dad's gonna kill me! What the hell are we going to do?"

Gavin is drunk and laughing.

And then, it happens. Again.

Every light on our block goes black, followed by the next block, and the next, and the next, until we are standing, staring at each other in the light of only the stars.

"Holy fuck," Mike concludes after a long, silent pause between the three of us.

We look towards the completely dark house, and I can see someone inside light up a flashlight through the living room window. They start moving through the house with the light, and through the open window, we can hear faint murmurs coming from the confused guests.

"Man! What did you do?" Gavin calls to Mike in a hushed voice. With a look of sheer panic on his face, he clutches his bag tightly in his left hand.

I pull out a small flashlight from my pocket and order the guys to follow me. They don't argue.

They follow me into the garage where I hope we can hide for a few minutes before the car is discovered, and I can make an alternate plan for a vehicle. We all stand in the dark and cluttered space between a shelf of old paint cans and a dusty treadmill, and I finally reach for Gavin's bag. He pulls it back towards his chest.

"I need to show you something. *Now.*"

His grip and posture soften at the urgency in my voice, and still somewhat hesitantly hands the bag over to me. I unzip the front pocket and hold out the torn beer box towards Mike. He looks at me with his arms crossed, looks down at the cardboard and then back up at my face. After staring at me for a few seconds angrily, he snatches the makeshift note from my hand and reads the scribble on the back.

Mike's eyes then return to mine and we stare at each other for what feels like hours. There are more murmurs from inside, so Gavin interrupts our stare down.

"Look, we need to get the hell out of here," he whispers, "We can walk to my house and borrow my Mom's car. We'll come up for a plan about the Camry and— "

"How did you know this?" Mike's tone is low and serious.

"I told you, I knew exactly what was going to happen because I'm—I've been here. Not literally here in this garage though. Last time you guys were already on your way to that party."

"Last time?"

"When I was actually fifteen. During the blackout. Thirteen years ago."

"I—you—but—if this is true—which it's not...How?"

"I don't know. But we've gotta get out of here before people notice the car. Or we're all fucked."

"Let's go," Mike exits the garage side door and doesn't give us a chance to argue. We follow quickly and quietly. When we get through the patch of trees in our backyard I flip the flashlight back on.

We enter Gavin's pitch-black house silently. Gavin's mom is asleep in her room and luckily is blissfully unaware of the blackout. He leaves her a note and takes the car keys from the hook, handing them to me. Mike starts to intervene but is silenced by a look from Gavin. He pops open another beer on the walk to the car and hands it to Mike who takes a big swig and hands it back. I still don't know where they think we're going, but this is much easier than I thought it would be.

Gavin's mom's car smells like vanilla and stale cigarettes. The smell triggers a memory—she dies of lung cancer in several years. I didn't go to the funeral, but my mom told me in an email. I feel a pang of guilt and look back at Gavin. He's in the backseat, sitting like a little kid with his feet up on the seat, reading the cardboard that's resting on his bony knees.

"This is unreal. You knew the exact time of the blackout? What else happens in the future? Dude, we're gonna be rich—let's go bet on some shit in Vegas or something."

Mike stays quiet and stares out the car window, marveling, "The whole damn city is out."

Gavin keeps rambling a drunken teenage flight of ideas, "Kendall, do I hook up with Tasha tonight? Who am I kidding, of course I do! Let's go bet on, like, the Laker's game or something this weekend—"

"You make a left up here," Mike directs me.

Gavin continues, "—but if we fuck with stuff, we're gonna end up in some kind of alternate, terrible universe. Oh, God, I don't want my kids to go to jail—"

"Ken, it's a left here!"

I drive past the turn towards Tasha's parents' house and take the exit towards downtown.

"Where the fuck are we going now?" Mike asks, throwing his hands up.

Gavin continues to debate with himself in the back seat, as I keep driving towards the office building that I remember going to so many years ago for *Take Your Daughter To Work* day.

—

Getting into the office building is surprisingly easy when you have nothing to lose. And when the power is out in the whole city. The automatic locks are off and there's no one at the security desk. The huge lobby is both eerily silent and completely empty. Gavin and Mike follow me in, staying a few paces back. They are so quiet and serious that they are barely recognizable. As I approach the elevator bank, the button is black, and I now realize this complication—*Without power, there are no elevators.*

Starting to panic, I run towards the stairwell on the opposite side of the lobby, opening the door and trying to get myself to calm down as I rationalize my way out of this situation. The power outage didn't last all night. I force the guys to follow me up the stair bank to the second floor, and I sit on the concrete landing, put the flashlight on its end pointing up to the ceiling, and wait.

"So are you gonna tell us why we broke into Dad's building?"

"Is this where your time machine is?" Gavin asks, excitedly.

"Gavin, why do you act like an idiot all the time? I know you got into Yale, you jackass," I snap as I snatch the bag out of his hand again and grab a room temperature beer. I hold my nose and chug it down.

"Yale?" Mike asks, "I thought you were going to Boulder with me."

"I—I haven't decided yet."

"He does go to Boulder, Mike. He got into Yale—he doesn't go," I pause, my arms crossed, waiting for Gavin to try to deny it.

When he finally speaks, his voice is small, "How did you know I got into Yale? I didn't even tell my Mom yet."

We are all silent for longer than I thought was possible.

"I thought we never talk in the *future,*" Mike says with air-quotes, "so how do you know that?"

"Facebook."

"What the fuck is—"

The power comes back on with a very loud thud followed by a whooshing sound. We all stare at the stairwell door, frozen. In the dim light of the flashlight, I had forgotten they were just kids. Mikes sandy brown hair is disheveled on his head and his eyes are red. Gavin's eyes are missing their usual glimmer as he scans the bank of stairs, his face a graphic novel of terror.

I realize I have a chance to break for it, and so I run out the door to the second floor and press the elevator button no less than a dozen times in rapid succession. The motor whirrs for about twenty seconds and pauses. I slam my palm against the button again for good measure, and, glancing back over my shoulder, I see two teenagers jogging towards me, one with a backpack. The elevator doors finally open, and I jump in before the doors start to close. Slowing to a walk, Mike and Gavin stare back at me from across the small lobby, their faces full of confusion and something that reminds me of worry. I smooth my hair and rub my index finger over my front teeth, then I push the button quickly as the doors shut between us. It's completely silent, and I am finally alone again. I look at my reflection in the shiny metal of the elevator door and for the first time I see my brother's blue eyes in my own. I shake my head in an attempt to clear it and watch the numbers light up: *3, 4, 5, 6, 7...*

I didn't realize I accidentally pushed *21* until it was too late.

12
YEAR 21

KENDALL

The elevator doors open, and a deep bass beat thumps around me, filling the small metal space and reverberating through my body. There are strobed silhouettes of people in the distance, seeming to grind on each other in slow motion. Looking around, it's hard to get my bearings because the only lights illuminating the area are colored, flashing, or surrounded by a foggy haze. I step out of the elevator despite my better judgment and trip over a ledge, catching myself on some kind of metal rail before I hit what appears to be a concrete floor. Rubbing my now sweaty palms on my thighs, I look down at my legs and notice I'm wearing four-inch heels and tight white pants. Scanning upward, my outfit is complete with a tight, sparkled black top and a push-up bra. I grip the railing harder until my knuckles match my pants—pants that now spark a familiar memory—and my face flushes with anger and regret.

From the hoard of dark bodies on what I now realize is a dance floor, a creepy guy materializes in the colored strobe light. He stares at me, smiles, and heads in my direction. I instinctively begin to back up, but I am nearly knocked onto my ass again as someone from behind me grabs my arm and pulls me backwards into the ladies' room.

"O-M-G, did you see that hot-ass bartender? He told me he liked my shirt. I think he was hitting on me."

I am unable to speak. The girl who grabbed me is now looking into the mirror and I'm standing off to the side behind her, both of us staring at her reflection.

"Uh, Courtney?"

"C'mon it was so obvious," my Sasquatch-turned-supermodel childhood friend says while applying charcoal eyeliner under both eyes and smudging it into oblivion. She has to bend slightly at the waist to see into the mirror that is too short for her. Her long platinum-blonde hair falls almost into the sink, framing her overly tan face that just has a hint of adolescent acne left on it. Her long legs are also super tan and bare, and she tugs down on a shiny black skirt that hardly covers them. As she turns to face me, I see why the bartender may have liked her top, as it leaves very little to the imagination. She catches me staring, and her face turns from self-satisfied to concerned, "Kendall, what's wrong?"

"Nothing. I'm just—I think I'm going to be sick," I turn away from her and dive into a stall behind me, luckily which is unoccupied, and throw up. After I have nothing left in my stomach, I spit into the filthy toilet and grab for some toilet paper to wipe my mouth, sitting back on my heels. Courtney stands over me with her mouth open and the eyeliner in her hand. Her face is now even more concerned and also disappointed, as she bends down to sit across from me on the bathroom floor. She reaches out to push my hair back behind my shoulder, and I recoil.

"No, don't sit. It's gross," I stand up, brushing myself off, and go over to the sink to wash my hands and rinse out my mouth.

Courtney gets back up and follows me to the sink. She smiles at me and asks, "Puke and rally?"

After I've washed my hands twice, I use a paper towel to turn off the faucet and ball it up in my hands, "Actually, can we please get out of here and go somewhere quieter? I really need to—"

"Hell no! We are bringing home some guys tonight! Hot guys! Fuck Chris and his stupid 'life-plan'! You are getting laid!"

Chris? Life Plan? Oh God—I feel the chunks rise up in my throat again. I swallow and pat the back of my neck with the damp, balled up paper towel.

Chris was my college boyfriend and the closest reference point I have to love. Nearly two years into our relationship, he was accepted into med school in Boston, which was a tremendous opportunity for him. It was one of the best programs in the country. After we celebrated his accomplishment with his parents at one of the swankiest restaurants in Manhattan, on a crowded subway car, he turned to me and said that it had been wonderful being with me but our careers were pulling us in different directions. That we both had life plans that were bigger than us. And I agreed, but still I wanted it to be my idea. I wanted it to be harder for him. But it just wasn't.

You are so great, he said clutching the filthy silver handle above our heads and speaking loudly over the other passengers, like they didn't matter. Like *I* didn't matter. *You are going to be such an amazing 'food-person' and I don't want my dream to get in your way.*

Fuck you, is all I could say before I got off in the train at the next stop and realized I had no one to call. No one to cry to. In my impulsive emotional state, I called Courtney.

In my calendar of memory, that was seven years ago. Now, I guess it was only a few weeks.

After applying some lip gloss, Courtney grabs my arm and drags me with her again, this time towards the bar. She hands me a fizzy pink drink and my hands are shaking so badly that I can hardly take a sip. Unaware of my unstable state, she shamelessly makes fuck-me eyes at the bartender, who clearly has no idea she exists and is busy mixing drinks and ignoring other patrons. I manage to get a sip of the pink drink into my mouth, which puckers at the terrible taste- something along the lines of burning grain alcohol and too-sweet lollipops. I put the mostly full plastic cup back on the bar and decide it's probably best to be clear-headed if I am going to prevent past mistakes. My stomach churns again at this thought.

Prevent past mistakes. Prevent past mistakes.

The words bounce around my head like the heavy thumping of the music.

I can't be here, on this night, again.

I start to back up from the bar and move towards the exit without Courtney noticing. I get a few paces back and stop, looking at the crowd of people swarming the bar like desperate animals.

Then, Gavin enters my mind, and I think for a moment about his blabbering in the backseat—*What if I change too much, and create a totally different, even more screwed-up universe? What if I decide not to follow Courtney to that apartment tonight and my life ceases to exist? Or when I finally get back to my life, I'm working at a Walmart and living with my parents?*

So to avoid a catastrophic misstep which could potentially alter the entire course of time, I make a plan to continue with the same path and only change things as minimally as possible. I straighten my posture and take a deep breath, stepping back towards Courtney. After I stand behind her silently for a few seconds and talk myself down from a full-blown panic attack, my heart sinks once again as I finally see the Asshole at the corner of the bar. At first, my memory of him is hazy, probably out of self-preservation, but the reality of him suddenly comes back at me like a rip current, pulling me out of control faster and stronger than I can ever try to return.

The Asshole is talking to a girl who's so disinterested in him that she literally turns her back as he's still talking. His gelled hair spiked out towards the ceiling, baggy jeans and shell necklace are all suddenly exactly as I remember them. He continues to speak to the girl, motioning to the bartender for a refill and still managing to look smug despite his obvious shut-down. Then his eyes scan the length of the bar, meeting mine for a moment. He then bounces his gaze back to Courtney as if he is calculating his odds. He half-smiles and creeps towards us just like before. My spine tingles and my heart races. Everything in me wants to punch him in the face and run in the opposite direction, but instead I smile and act like my naive twenty-one-year-old self. But as he approaches, before he even speaks, there is a very subtle change in my memory of the night. The Asshole glances down at my drinkless hands and instead passes his attention fully to an alternative victim. *Courtney.*

13

MIKE

We drive down Route 36 in silence, passing the bowl back and forth, and I can't really find the right thing to say. Words pop into my head, but they disappear before I can think of anything reassuring.

I slowly pull onto the exit ramp towards the airport, and a giggle escapes my mouth as I find a spot to stop in front of departures, "I'll pick you up when you get back," I manage to spit out in between chuckles.

"Okay," Gavin laughs, trying to smother his own explosion of laughter, "I can't remember when my flight back is, but I'm sure my dad will get me there. I mean, he's a dad."

We both crack up, and he grabs his backpack, gets out of the car and heads for the terminal. It's early enough in Denver that the sun is still not up, and the sky is painted with pink, orange, and yellow in preparation. I pull away from the airport and take the exit back towards our shitty apartment in Boulder without a thought in my head—just the way I prefer it.

14

KENDALL

After a thrilling conversation at the club about how great the DJ is, Courtney continues her descent into naive victim and insists we go back to his apartment to continue drinking. I follow suit, so as not to disrupt the chronology of my life, but it's painful for me to pretend like everything is fine. After several more drinks in our new location, the irresponsibles are now extremely wasted, which is good news for me because I no longer have to act like I want to be here. I can just wait it out until my cab comes, and I don't give a shit what happens to Courtney after that. I'll never see her again after tonight anyway.

I sip a lukewarm hard lemonade so that I don't have to speak and pretend to be listening to the Asshole tell some story about his car. He stands in the middle of the living room, eyes half closed and drunkenly swaying in emphasis when he gets to an important word like 'exhaust' or 'cunt'. Courtney gazes up at him, enthralled with the story and giggling like a drunk school-girl. I have to look away because I am afraid I might throw the nearly full lemonade at his gelled head. Or maybe at his chest, that way it could ruin his too-tight graphic T-shirt that shows off his shaved arms. As he wraps up the story, he returns to his seat next to Courtney on the overstuffed black leather sofa, and she drapes her foot over his thigh. He scoots his torso over towards her and she puts her hand over his waist until they are basically sitting on the same couch cushion. I feel another twinge in my gut to knee him in the balls at this very moment in front of everyone, but I worry about the cosmic repercussions and decide it's best to just wait it out. We all watch his roommate play a terrible rendition of Black Sabbath on *Guitar Hero*, and I check my phone over and over again for a missed call from the cab company.

Courtney pops up from the black hole of a couch and announces that she has to pee. She looks at Asshole with a slight nod and he follows her into the back of the apartment. I am left with the Roommate who is now passed out, mid guitar solo, on a recliner. Perched on my own love seat, I'm trying to wait it out until my cab arrives, but patience has never been one of my strengths. I check the time on my phone, and oddly enough, Asshole is right on schedule. The only difference is his victim. I hear a toilet flush and a door open in the back of the apartment.

My sober, twenty-eight-year-old brain is not much help to me right now. Last time I was here, drunk and naive, I did not have the clarity or the sense that I have at this moment. I sit on the edge of the sticky, faux leather love seat, bouncing my knee to the back beat of the video game that is now stuck in a loop, and I'm now taking part in a full-blown internal war with my conscience. Counting the seconds, I watch the fake guitar chords scroll on the screen in front of us, and I am fucking pissed off at the part of me that appears to be winning.

I am not going back there. I am not going back there. I am not going back there.

After the sound of another door shutting, I finally give in to my inner voice, and, wrapping my purse strap across my chest, I approach the back of the apartment without knowing quite how I am going to do this. In a sudden impulse, I grab an Axe body spray from off of the bathroom sink and barge into the Asshole's bedroom. Courtney is naked and in a compromising position on the bed, and she doesn't appear to be moving or even awake. Asshole is rummaging through a drawer next to his bed, so he doesn't hear me coming until the sudden hissing sound of the dirty frat-boy chemicals leaves the can. That smell that is forever burned into my memory. He falls to the floor, clutching his eyes and screaming.

"You fucking BITCH!"

I turn to run out of the bedroom alone, and in a split second of weakness, I force myself to turn back around. I dodge Asshole as he runs past me to the bathroom, and I grab the closest item of clothing and shove it over Courtney's head. She's barely conscious but asks me what I'm doing in a weak voice.

"The bartender is waiting for us," I tell her in a hushed voice as fast as I possibly can, "hurry, he might leave, we've gotta go meet him outside."

She wobbles onto her feet and stumbles over to what appears to be her purse. I grab it before she can, while also grabbing her under the arm, and shove her towards the door. I hear the faucet running in the bathroom and cabinet doors slamming, one after another, all interspersed with stomping and cursing. I have no idea what he's capable of, but before we find out my adrenaline helps me drag Courtney's semi-conscious body out of the apartment and down the stairs to the parking lot.

And then, something shifts within me. An inexplicable softness envelopes my mind but also sharpens it. My phone starts to ring. I see the cab waiting for us across the parking lot. I hear shouting and stomping from behind us, now getting closer and closer, and I throw the car door open, shoving Courtney and her purse into the back of the cab. I bark at the driver to take us to the only address I can remember, and we speed away from this version of this terrible night.

15

MIKE

With Gavin gone the days seem way longer than usual. There's only so much PlayStation 3 one man can play solo. After couching for several hours, I survey the mess around me and decide maybe I'll clean up a little. After all, there's nothing better to do.

I grab a garbage bag and start throwing out the first layer of trash on the floor. I toss Gavin's clothes that are all over the apartment into a giant pile on the floor in his room. His uniform from PriceMart is balled up on his desk. There's no way I'm touching that—dude thinks because snow is frozen water that snowboarding counts as a shower.

Something weird is going on with me. Not only am I cleaning the apartment, but I also have an endless stream of thoughts running through my head without my idiot roommate to distract me. A normal off-season Saturday with Gavin typically consists of a wake-and-bake sesh, some *Grand Theft Auto*, grabbing a burrito and a case of beer, and by then it's time to get dressed and mack at the bars near campus. Without him, I'm stuck here weedless and thinking. Celeste pops into my mind, and then I can't stop thinking about Sunnyvale. I got out of there as fast as I could after high school, thank God. But now I can't kick the 'what if' thoughts out of my head.

I blame social media for this kind of shit. Until they freaking 'suggested' friends for me, I had not even thought twice about these people from back home.

"How's your sister?" Gavin asked last Thursday when I told him I accepted some bullshit Facebook friend of hers from high school, Caitlin—no, Courtney.

"No fucking clue, man."

Normally it would piss me off that he asked about my bitch-of-a-sister at all, which he knows after I beat the shit out of him Junior year when he called her hot, but I'm distracted by a new message in my inbox.

Hey Stranger, it starts. I slam the laptop shut and tell myself not to re-open it. I know it's from her.

I move to the other side of the room, shoving my lacrosse stick into my closet, and my poncho falls down from the top shelf. I pick it up and remember the day that I broke up with Celeste—the same day my sister went mental. It's a day I try hard to forget but Gavin has a tendency to bring up when he's blackout. After that day, Kendall finished her progression from snotty little sister into a complete stuck-up bitch. She acted like nothing happened and started treating me like I was a complete fuck-up, instead of just a partial one.

I wouldn't even know she lived in New York if my mom didn't insist on calling me once a week to cry about why Kendall didn't return her phone calls.

God, women are freaking nuts.

I shove my poncho back up onto the shelf and my hand hits some glass. I reach as far back as I can, fumbling around, and grab a bottle.

"Well, hello, old friend."

I open the half-empty fifth of shitty whiskey and take a big swig.

16

KENDALL

I wake up to the sun streaming through pink floral curtains and melodic snoring coming from the trundle bed beneath me. I ease out of bed, careful not to step on Courtney as I slip between the end of the bed and the dresser, and rummage through my old drawers for a pair of sweatpants. The smell of bacon and coffee wafts under the bedroom door, enticing me to enter the third ring of hell downstairs. I note to myself that there's at least one good thing about being twenty-one again—I can wake up after being out until three AM and feel great.

I shuffle into the kitchen and my dad's sitting at the counter reading the paper. My mom is standing over the stove cooking eggs and bacon. Neither of them looks up when I head to the fridge for some diet cranberry juice. I pull out the jug and read the ingredients.

Crap, this kind isn't made with Stevia—I can't drink this aspartame death-juice.

I close the fridge and sigh audibly in frustration.

"Good morning, Kendall," my mom says in a flat tone without looking up from the skillet, "We didn't know you were back from school."

I start on my prepared bullet points—"Mom, I told you a month ago I'd be back for fall break."

"I thought you couldn't stay with us because of your 'very important' conference?"

Shit. Already a deviation?

I suddenly remember that I lied about having a conference to go to, and so I never came home this break. I had to come back to the west coast one last time for my stuff, but there was no way in hell I was staying with my parents for a full week. I think I ended up meeting them in San Francisco for brunch, and even that two hours was torture. My plan of keeping things the same seems to be unraveling a bit.

"The keynote speaker pulled out at the last minute. Sorry I didn't tell you ahead of time, but I thought it would be a nice surprise," I say with forced smile. My mom finally looks up from the stove like she wants to say something to me, but then glances over my shoulder.

"Oh, hello, Courtney. It's been a long time. You look very—grown up."

Courtney's hair is a twisted nest, and her face has a few specks of crusted mascara and hair gel. She smiles weakly at my mom and doesn't look me in the eye, "Thanks Mrs. G. Do you mind if I have some coffee?"

"Not at all, sweetie. Help yourself."

The four of us silently eat our breakfast. I push my eggs around and nibble at them, but I really can't eat supermarket eggs. They taste like caged fear. As we sit in silence, I wonder what Courtney remembers from last night. After several long, silent minutes at the table, she looks at me with concern and excuses herself to my parents. Clutching her mouth, she walks briskly to the upstairs jack-and-jill bathroom that adjoins my room with Mike's. I thank my parents for the food and follow her across the house and up the stairs. I can feel their eyes watching me the whole time.

It's surreal being back here. I was just here 'yesterday' when I was fifteen, but today the vibe between my parents and I is drastically altered with, to me, what feels like only three hours. There's a pang of guilt in my stomach again—the same one that compelled me to intervene last night. I decide since Courtney is here, and I will soon have a very awkward drive back to her house, I may as well check on her. Get the awkwardness over with.

I knock very lightly on the bathroom door, "Courtney? Can I...get you something? Maybe some Perrier?"

"What?" she asks weakly.

I hear the toilet flush, and as a result I start to walk back to my old room to give her some space. Courtney opens the bathroom door between us. I turn around and her face is pale and streaked with tears.

I recoil from her vulnerability, instead choosing to turn around and hide back in my childhood bedroom. On top of figuring out how the hell I'm going to get back to my real life and out of this alternate-alternate universe, I don't have the time or energy to de-escalate a practical stranger. I just need to lure her out of the bathroom before my parents start asking too many questions.

I sit on my bed, staring at the pictures of the two of us that still line the walls of my room and try to think back to when we were friends. *What was Courtney like?*

In high school, I think she wanted to be a designer. She was obsessed with anything related to high fashion, and nearly got us both banned from Nordstrom drooling over the expensive shoe section. From age ten to age sixteen, a day did not pass without a lengthy phone call about clothes, boys, or reality TV stars. Then we started to grow apart between Junior and Senior year when Courtney left for a summer internship at the LA Fashion Institute, and I was still hanging around Sunnyvale bored and waiting for my acceptance to NYU. Having disappeared for most of the summer break, she returned for the start of senior year and was all everyone could talk about: how talented she was and how modelesque she was (Sasquatch was no longer). Instead of returning to our adolescent invisibility together, she blossomed and I filled the role of short, forgettable sidekick. I stopped calling her back on the weekends, and when we graduated and I finally moved to New York we would see each other maybe two or three times a year during school breaks. Semesters came and went, and then things sort-of flipped. I got a killer paid internship at *Bon Appetit*, and she had no job offers lined up. She had become a train-wreck, party-girl, and when we would see each other on rare occasions, I began to sense that she was now envious of me. I still maintained my role of 'plain jane' of the friendship in the physical sense, but now I was doing exciting things that she and everyone in Sunnyvale were not a part of. For God's sake, I think I have more than five thousand followers of my first blog by this age.

My bedroom door slowly creaks open and half of Courtney appears in the doorway, "Did I have sex with that guy?" she whimpers, looking down at her hands.

"Probably," I say matter-of-factly.

"What do you mean *probably*?" she moves towards me and closes the door behind her, "Did you hear us?"

"No. Not exactly."

"Kendall, please," she looks me directly in the eye. For a second I think I might try to comfort her, and give her a reassuring pat on the shoulder, but instead I get up and rush through the explanation while gathering my stuff.

"Alright. He tried, I think. You were really wasted, and I heard things that didn't sound right, and I know his M-O, and I decided to intervene."

"His *M-O*? What?"

"I mean—I know someone that he—took advantage of. Before. In the past. And I wasn't going to let that happen to anyone else. So I sprayed the Asshole in the face with some cheap body spray and we left."

And then without warning she hugs me, leaning down and locking her arms around my stiff shoulders, her chest heaving with sobs. I just stand still and let her cry. Courtney isn't trying to one-up me or casting her shadow over me at the moment—she's just hungover and sad. Even a few months ago, I still felt that underlying envy while scrolling through her beautiful Instagram photos of her college girls smiling over lattes or showing off their new bikinis on the beach. But that's not what our reality is right now.

As she begins to breathe normally, she pulls away and uses the inside of her shirt hem to wipe her face. I busy myself with packing a bag and changing into jeans and the first T-shirt I can find. I don't want to talk or even think about last night anymore—I already had to live two terrible versions of it.

We are both silent as I drive Courtney back to her house, which is a few neighborhoods away. I pull my dad's Volvo into the driveway but she pauses before opening her passenger door, looking back over at me.

"If you're in town next weekend, I'm doing this show to benefit lung cancer research—"

"Sorry I have to get back," I assert, my eyes on the steering wheel.

"Okay," she says in a tone that's somewhere between surrender and sadness. She gets out of the car but stops and turns back to look at me again, the door ajar, "Thank you, Ken. You are a really good friend."

In all the years of our late adolescence that I spent riding around in Courtney's crappy Geo Tracker, drinking Sprite spiked with cheap vodka and trying to get boys to make-out with us so that we felt wanted, she never once said anything close to that. It makes me uncomfortable in an unfamiliar way, so I choose to keep moving forward and not to acknowledge it.

"Well, good luck with your show."

"Thanks. See you later."

I look down and put the car in reverse as she walks up to her house and enters. I quickly pull out of the driveway and don't look back.

Yet again, I need a revised plan. Looking at this from a Susan Wilder perspective—just because I got off at the wrong floor doesn't mean that my previous plan was completely unsuccessful, it just means there was a slight error with the procedure. Or I was too panicked and hit the wrong button. I am older and wiser in this year of my life, and now I have the foresight not to make that mistake again. And I have a driver's license and access to a car, which means less complications from idiot teenage boys. I turn at the next traffic light, feeling a sense of relief, and start along the main road, towards the distant skyline of San Jose.

—

After I've been driving for less than five minutes, I suddenly hear a long, high-pitched beep followed by several loud clunks, and the Volvo begins to slow. Regardless of how hard I slam the accelerator to the floor, the car does not gain speed, and people are starting to honk for me to get out of their way. I'm able to navigate the car at a slow creep over to the shoulder without getting hit from behind, and it crawls to a stop on the side of the road. Trying not to panic, I take a few deep breaths and then rummage around in my bag, remembering suddenly that I have my shitty phone that my parents bought me when I moved to New York. As I start to type in a search, the low battery warning blares at me and the screen goes black before I can load any information. I push the power button several times to no avail and then throw it down into the passenger seat floorboard as hard as I possibly can. Looking around, I recognize the building to my right as my old dentist's office, allowing me to estimate that I'm probably a mile or two from the closest gas station. For a split second I consider calling my dad, but that would involve a lecture and a lengthy explanation about why I had to leave immediately to get to the city. Besides, I'm better off just handling things on my own like usual.

I get out of the car brimming with anger. I slam the car door behind me, open the trunk, grab the spare gas tank, and slam the trunk shut again. I can feel frustration and fury building in every muscle of my body, and I can't take it anymore. I kick the back of the Volvo's bumper with all my might, and the force of my kick pushes the car forward about an inch, which is just enough of a sudden jolt to knock my dad's golf bag off of the back seat. In seemingly slow motion, a can of Old Spice spray deodorant rolls out of the bag and onto the floorboard of the car. I stare through the glass at the can for a few seconds, and like a maniac I rip the car door open, pick it up and hurl it at the asphalt as hard as I possibly can. The can makes a loud hissing sound but doesn't break. Unsatisfied by the damage, I stomp on it, over and over and over again, but it just dents and hisses back at me. Despite the fact that I'm on the side of a public road, with cars whizzing by me, in my mind there is nothing except my anger and this can.

"FUCK YOU! You fucking ASSHOLE!" I scream at the ground.

I can never be certain of what happened that night—the other version of last night—but there was blood and pain and shame the next morning. And really until this moment, I convinced myself it was my fault. After all, I went to the club in those tight white pants that would never be white again. And I liked it when he touched my leg and looked into my eyes and made me feel like I was desired. That desire, mixed with alcohol and fueled by heartbreak, made me forget that I barely knew the Asshole and follow him home to that same apartment. Courtney had encouraged it initially, until I left the bar without her, disappointment and jealousy scrawled across her drunken face.

I stomp the can again, the hissing louder than before. The bottom of the can feels like it's close to giving way—to exploding.

The next morning, in complete silence, Courtney drove me to the Planned Parenthood around the corner from our old high school and signed the paperwork while I threw up in the bathroom. When I emerged from the building with her, Plan B in hand, my eyes red from crying and throwing up, I heard a familiar voice in the parking lot, talking loudly on her cell phone and sucking down a cigarette.

—holy shit. Is that—

Ohmygod hurry up and get in the fucking car, I demanded to Courtney, under my breath, praying that my brother's ex-girlfriend Celeste would not see us.

It wasn't until a few days later that I discovered she undoubtedly did.

And the same 'concern' that led her to message my brother on Facebook to tell him, also apparently motivated my dick of a brother to tell my parents. And you can guess how that went. I practically ran back to New York and never ever looked back.

Stomp. Hiss.
Pop.

Always a disappointment.

My aerosol assault is interrupted by distant yelling from across the parking lot. At first, it's just an indistinguishable male voice, but then I can make out my name, "—Kendall!"

In a daze and out of breath, I look up towards the voice. Just past a small patch of grass and a guard rail is a parking lot, which is mostly empty. An old strip mall sits beyond the lot, with offices and storefronts that are in need of some maintenance. Near the edge of the parking lot, more than several yards away, I can see a woman in a wheelchair and a tall guy pushing her towards me.

"Kendall Gibbons? Mike's sister?" he shouts from the distance, "you okay?"

Still moving towards me, the two are a little closer now, and I can tell now that the guy is probably in his early twenties. The frail woman taps his arm, and he bends down to her level. I assume she says something in his ear, because he then locks the wheelchair in place and continues towards me without her. She waves at me knowingly and gives me a weak smile. The tall, now visibly strong guy with long tan arms, deep brown eyes, and a warm smile approaches me. He laughs and runs his hand through his dark brown, wavy hair.

"Oh, hey, Gavin," I say as I stand awkwardly with the Volvo keys in one hand and the gas tank in the other. I can feel sweat dripping from the nape of my neck down my back, and I look down at the mangled Old Spice can at my feet.

"Hey. You alright?" he looks at me, confused and clearly concerned, and then glances back at the woman to check on her. She has closed her eyes and put her head back to rest on the back of the wheelchair.

I just stare at him in a daze. I cannot think of a single good way to answer that question, and I'm relieved that he doesn't wait for me to.

"C'mon, I have my truck here—lemme drop off my mom and then I'll take you to a gas station."

Now that I've let all that anger out in an embarrassingly public display, I feel deflated and weak. And my mind is tired. I follow Gavin and his mom to his truck slowly, keeping a comfortable distance between us and trying not to stare at her gaunt cheekbones. I say a brief hello to his mom and climb into the bench seat in the back of the cab. Gavin then lifts her into the passenger seat like she's hollow, folds the wheelchair and puts it in the truck bed, and hops into the driver's seat. In the side mirror, I can see his mom dozing off as we drive down the tree-lined streets of the neighborhood. In the bright light of midday, her pale skin almost glows.

We pull up to their house, and the memories of this place come flooding back. This is where I spent many an afternoon as a small kid, trying to get Mike and Gavin to let me play with them. Gavin helps his mom out of the truck and walks her in, supporting most of her weight with his arm. I wait silently in the truck for several long minutes. The air conditioning feels good on my skin, and the smell is familiar and calming. I'm so exhausted and so comfortable that when I close my eyes I can almost forget the last forty-eight hours, and I lay my head back and seem to do just that.

I'm snapped back into my alternate reality with the sound of the driver's door opening and slamming shut quickly. Gavin fastens his seatbelt, adjusts himself in the seat and pulls his shorts down over a noticeable tan line, and I can't help staring at his legs, which are now filled out with more muscle and hair then I ever remember him having. He catches me looking and I awkwardly divert my eyes to my car window.

"So—" Gavin remarks, interrupting the uncomfortable silence "—what brings you back to town?"

"Um. I...well...it's fall break. I came to get my stuff. From my parents' house," I catch my reflection in the side mirror of his truck and am reminded that I look like a complete train wreck. I try to cover my face by resting my head on my arm that's propped up against the passenger window, "and I'm going back tonight," I add.

"Oh," he says, surprised, "where to?"

"Manhattan. I am graduating NYU this...uh...soon."

"Oh yea? I think Mike told me you were in New Jersey or New York or something. That's cool."

Another awkward silence ensues, and my brain takes off again in several different directions. I think about yesterday, when I spent the evening trying to convince him and Mike I was twenty-eight. It was seven years ago to him, if it really even happened in order—before this twenty first year.

"You were always writing those crazy plays and poems and stuff. Are you in school for that?"

I'm taken aback by the fact that he remembers this detail about me. I manage to stammer a response, "Writing? Well, sort of. I write a food blog. It's been featured in *Self Magazine*."

I cringe internally realizing that doesn't happen for four more years. But there's no way Gavin would know this anyway, so I breathe out in relief.

"That's pretty sweet...I love food," he looks at me and chuckles awkwardly. I try to stifle a laugh but it comes out as a snort. I turn beet-red, mortified.

Gavin laughs at me a little too hard in response, but then when he notices my embarrassment, he smirks, "Sorry."

"Apology not accepted," I say with a half-smile back to him and we meet eyes for an instant until I am the first to look away.

We finally pull into the gas station. He reaches down and grabs the gas can that I had resting on the floorboard, propped between my feet, and his arm brushes my knee as I try to shift and get out of his way. I feel a strange feeling in the pit of my stomach, like someone flipped me upside down and back again. When I look back up from my legs, he's already turned to get out of the truck and I'm alone. I resort to distracting myself by planning out my next blog topic for my return to normalcy: Free range eggs. I clutch my stomach which I'm sure is probably just reacting to my mom's crappy breakfast food and try focus on my next steps towards getting into that elevator tonight. I should get a move on already, since after business hours it's gonna be a lot more difficult to convince the security guards that I have a legitimate reason to be there.

"Alright let's hope your car's still there," Gavin says, returning with his goofy smile and starting up the truck again.

"What? Why wouldn't it be? Would someone steal it? Oh, God, did I leave it unlocked? Oh my gosh, I didn't even put the hazards on! What if someone hit it?"

Gavin puts his hands up and brings them back down in a 'settle down' motion, looking at me with his now wide brown eyes, "Whoa, whoa—chill. I was just joking...I'm sure it's fine. It's Saturday—there's hardly anyone on the road," he laughs at me in a familiar way, driving me crazy as he and Mike did back in the day.

We pull up to my dad's car and I get out, walk around to the driver's door and open it, realizing that I actually did leave the door unlocked. In my entire adult life, I don't think I have ever left a car, house, or apartment door unlocked. *Haven't you seen CSI?*

While I am distracted by my uncharacteristic negligence with the car, Gavin takes it upon himself to put the gas in the tank.

"This will get you a few miles but you need to go to a gas station and fill 'er up the rest of the way," he says, tapping the top of the rear roof with his knuckle. I notice his ring finger is empty, but then remind myself that he's probably only like twenty-three years old.

We both pause and he looks me directly in the eye. I hold his gaze for a moment, wondering what he's thinking, and then look away.

Trying to be cordial, I smile and impulsively make conversation, "Since when are you Mr. Responsible, saving the day, planning ahead and stuff?"

"Ah, shut up," he smiles, "I've always been fairly responsible."

"Oh yea, you never forgot to bring the beer once. That's true," I smirk.

"You're welcome for rescuing you, Kendall," he says, still smiling as he takes a few strides towards me and hands the gas can over. I'm forced to look up at him when we are this close together, since he's at least seven or eight inches taller than me. I notice he's filled out since I saw him yesterday at age seventeen, mostly with muscle. Our eyes meet again, and I realize that all this time of riding in his truck and I didn't ask him a single question about his life.

"Does your mom have cancer?" I suddenly blurt out, knowing the answer and immediately wanting to crawl under something large and heavy. My face feels hot and now I remember why I don't make small talk.

"Yes," he says matter-of-factly.

"Do you still live in Sunnyvale?"

"Nah."

"Why are you here?"

"My dad's out of town and she's going through another round of chemo. Needs someone to drive her back and forth to the doctor."

"Oh."

There's another long, awkward pause. I decide I need an excuse to leave. I don't know why I've continued this conversation even this long.

"You want to grab a beer? I have to head back home in an hour or two but we could go get a beer and catch up?" Gavin asks innocently, "wait, you're twenty-one, right?"

I glance down at my phone and it's already three thirty. I have to get downtown and find that elevator soon or I might end up stuck here another night.

"I really have to get going. I have a meeting downtown at, um, four. Er, four-thirty, I mean. It's important."

Luckily Gavin is not one for details and thus doesn't press me for more information.

"There's a cool bar with a patio a few exits down the Five," he smiles and apparently doesn't take a hint.

I remark internally that Gavin did just save me more than an hour of walking back and forth to the gas station. For that, I could buy him a beer. And maybe I could find out more about his life in Boulder and what's happened to Mike.

"Okay. Let me go use the bathroom and I'll follow you there."

MIKE

Flashes of recollection— A dirty couch. Cups and beer cans lining the coffee table, end table, dining table. Dim lights and smoke. Music thumping and people in every corner of the cluttered house.

I am at a party. I think I've been here before.

The room spins and a memory of her pops back into my mind. She's laying with her cheek on my chest and laughing, her beautiful blonde hair draped across my torso. I throw the memory back out again. Another shot of whiskey and she'll disappear—I'm sure of it.

The music pauses for a moment as someone switches the song on the stereo and a giant hand slaps me on the back.

"Mike! Take a fucking hit with me brother!"

I press the bowl to my lips and breathe in the sweet burning air, just like I'm instructed by some dude I just met that has become my new best friend. Well, for tonight at least.

The spinning is worse now, but the most unfortunate side effect of weed is that my thoughts become more pronounced and Celeste is now all I can think about.

Hey Stranger...

I loved her. I wish I hadn't but against my better judgment, I did. And she was not in love with me. And it's been six damn years of remembering only the good things about her. Which in reality were likely very minimal compared to the shitty, manipulative parts.

I have always been a sucker for hot girls and so here I sit, stoned and drunk, waiting for her to message me back. Refreshing my phone like a fucking pussy.

Driving to Boulder with my boyfriend this weekend and would love to catch up...

—

"I'm so glad we could do this," she says, hugging me with one arm, the other on her coffee cup. My head pounds from my hangover, the taste of liquor and weed still lingering in the back of my throat. I may feel like shit, but I showered and put on my best shirt. I order a coffee that I don't intend on drinking and motion towards an outdoor table. Boulder is still sleepy after a late college night of festivities. The street is quiet with only an occasional passing car. Celeste looks really good, but she is more ordinary than she used to be. Her body is still amazing, but her blonde hair is more dull than I remember, and her skin is this dry, unnatural orange color. We sit at the wrought iron weathered table in front of the coffee shop and she immediately lights up a cigarette. She used to look cool and sexy smoking but now she's just kind of old and tired looking. Like smoking's something that's become an obligation rather than a privilege.

"So I ran into your sister's friend Courtney back home," she takes a puff and exhales through her nostrils, "And she offered me a modeling gig. But she also wanted me to talk to you because she really needs people to come to the show."

"Why the hell would she want you to talk to me?"

"Because she wants people to understand the importance of the fundraiser or something—it's for lung cancer victims."

"That's ironic."

She puts out her cigarette with a smirk, flipping her hair back with her other hand and looking up at me with those flirtatious eyes of hers.

"I'm just walking in the show to diversify my portfolio, alright? I'm not under some obligation to give a shit about the cause."

And there it is. She's still a terrible human being.

"How noble of you."

She keeps her eyes down on her fingers, tapping the ash onto the patio, "Anyway, I think she wants you to ask Gavin, you know, if his mom would be in it. I told her I knew you and when I was in town I'd drop by and try to talk to you guys about it."

"So, let me get this right—you're hoping to exploit Gavin and his mom to increase the credibility of your modeling portfolio?"

"God, I forgot how much of a dick you are," she gets up, putting her cigarette out, and turns, starting to walk away.

I get up and follow after her, watching her stomp away from me, a few steps behind. Her hips sway in that confident air she always exuded, making her go from average to hot in an instant. She glances back at me with a glare, and what feels like a subtle invitation and turns the corner into an alley. I turn the corner after her, and she is standing there, looking at me with that hunger that

I also feel in every inch of my body. I close the gap between us with a few slow paces towards her and she kisses me, pulling me intensely against her, so that we both fall against the side of the building, grabbing at each other in desperation. It takes every ounce of my energy, but I manage to pull myself away and out of the embrace before we start ripping off our clothes. I lean against the wall and look at her, as she wipes the corner of her mouth and straightens her skirt.

"Celeste, what are you doing?"

"I told you—"

"You have a boyfriend. And we're terrible for each other."

"He's not monogamous, so I'm not either."

"Sounds promising," I retort as I straighten the top of my collared shirt, "I guess some things never change."

Her eyes lose their sparkle as she looks down at herself and back up at me. The endlessly confident girl from my past seems to now have a veil of insecurity that's hard to pinpoint, but it's definitely there.

"Look, can you just talk to Gavin so she'll get off my back? The girl is fucking relentless on social media, and I'm afraid she'll piss off my followers."

"Yea, alright. Fine. But he's not around this weekend."

17

KENDALL

I look at myself in the dirty, warped mirror of the gas station bathroom, and I'm even more of a mess than I thought I was. My golden-brown hair is tied up in a knot on top of my head with rogue pieces of greasy hair popping out in every direction, and old mascara is caked under my eyes. I have sweat stains on my shirt, which I think must've belonged to my dad a decade ago and is two sizes too big. I pull my hair out of the knot, and it cascades down over my shoulders in long waves. I smooth it down and try to tame the craziness a bit. Later this year, I'll get my hair cut off to my chin and dye it blonde. Long hair was way too complicated to style in the morning and too easily appears unprofessional. I use what's left of the toilet paper to wipe the black smudges from under my green eyes and pinch my cheeks to bring some color back into my face. Out of everything my mother gave me, my high cheekbones are the only thing I've been happy to keep. I rummage through my purse quickly, finding some eyeshadow and lip gloss, likely thanks to my night at the club. The results are a slight improvement.

The bar Gavin chooses is actually fairly quiet and unassuming, which is extremely unexpected coming from my brother's dufus of a best friend. This is a guy who spends the majority of his waking hours stoned and playing video games. Or did when I knew him, at least.

"Sorry this place is kind of lame right now. Later on there's usually live music and the atmosphere is way better."

I stop him, "Look. I'm sorry, I can't really stay very long. I'll buy you a beer for picking me up, but then I'm heading out."

"Just sit down and I'll get you a drink," he says confidently.

"No, Gavin, I—"

He walks away and leaves me at an outdoor table. I sit for a moment, and then my mind starts up again. *I have got to get out of here. I'm wasting time.*

I get up and quickly make my way through the tables, as Gavin comes jogging towards me with two beers.

"Hey! You trying to take off on me?"

"No, I, I...forgot to lock the car."

"Seems to be a recurring issue with you," he grins, and tilts his beer back, taking a big swig, "Mike has the opposite problem."

"What, he locks his car too frequently?" I snap, "Look I really have to get back—"

"No—he just doesn't worry so much about details and so he can be kinda forgetful," he pauses and adds, "Gets him in trouble sometimes, but Mike isn't just a fuck-up like you think he is."

I stop and turn to face him, "Oh, yeah? That's good news for him."

"He's got a job, and an apartment—give the man some credit."

"What, a job at PriceMart as a cart boy? That's all he's qualified for."

"No. Home Depot. But I work at PriceMart, and I'm not a fucking cart boy thank you very much. I'm a stock boy," he smiles.

I blush and look down at my feet, simultaneously embarrassed that I insulted him and also frustrated that he's still so freaking up-beat about it.

"We all can't have our shit together all the time. Just give him a break."

I start to formulate my rebuttal about setting goals and working towards them, and for some unknown reason, I stop myself. His eyes lock with mine and it catches me off guard.

"You know, when he's really wasted, he brings up that night a lot."

"Sounds like a non 'fuck-up' thing to do," I add sarcastically.

"I'm serious."
"What night?"
"You know what night."
I don't say anything. So he remembers yesterday. It happened in the past of this past, sort of. I try to think of the first of a million questions I have.
"What does he say about it?"
"That it was fucking crazy."
"And that's it?"
"No, I mean, also that we wished we had done mushrooms with you that night. Would've been sweet," he laughs.
"I've never taken drugs."
"When the security guard picked you up out of the elevator, you were zonked. You can't tell me you weren't on something."
"Someone picked me up? How did I get home?"
"Your parents came to the emergency room and got you. You were still passed out. How did they not tell you this?"
"What happened after that?"
"You acted like nothing ever happened."
"We never talked about it?"
"Um, no. Have we ever really talked since? You barely talked to Mike before we left for Boulder."
So nothing else really changed. My brother and I still don't give a shit about each other.

Mike and I stopped talking after I moved to New York. He didn't call me, and after long enough, I didn't care to find out why. I'm across the country making something of myself, and he simply does not understand how important goals are. This thought reminds me that it's time for me to get back to my life that I worked hard to create for myself.

"Thanks for the gas. And the ride. I have to get to my appointment now."
Gavin is noticeably annoyed, "Kendall, nobody's perfect. And bad shit happens in life, even to people who always do the right thing. Look at my mom. Fucking terminal lung cancer."
"Gavin, I'm—"

He puts up his hand to stop me. I've never seen Gavin this serious before. I have a strong urge to hold him and tell him everything will be okay. But I can't lie to him.

"I believed you, about the blackout," he added, "so did Mike for a little while."

"And now?"

"Doesn't matter. Haven't seen you in six years anyway."

I pause. "What if I told you it didn't feel like six years to me?"

"Yea, okay—"

"It was yesterday."

He looks at me like I'm insane, which I very well might be, and I finally can sense some fatigue in his gaze. He rubs his forehead, "What the hell are you talking about?"

"My plan didn't work. I ended up here. Instead of where I came from. Twenty-one instead of twenty-eight."

"You really are mental, aren't you?" he laughs.

"I have to go try again. That's where I'm going. Back to the elevator."

"So you're telling me you're from the future?" he smirks.

"I don't know. My mind is twenty-eight. I have all the memories and experiences of twenty-eight years of life. I have no idea what that means but I definitely don't belong in a fifteen-year-old or twenty-one-year-old body."

"Well...what happens in the next seven years then?"

"It's not the seven years that are important—that was all a stepping stone. My life is about to actually start. I have an opportunity to be who I always dreamed I'd be," I pause and look at him, "You wouldn't get it."

"You think I don't have dreams? That I'm just a worthless stoner with a dead-end job?"

"I never said you were worthless."

This time he's not smiling, "Well, fuck off then. Go be whoever you think you want to be. Don't give a shit about anyone else besides yourself and have a great fucking life."

He walks towards his truck and doesn't look back. I see his hands clench into tight fists before he slams the door and takes off. I'm confused and angry, and compoundingly confused about why I am angry. I try to shake off the negative feelings by doing what I have to do—I get gas, I get in the car, and I formulate my next steps in my head. But my mind keeps drifting back to the last twenty minutes, and I can't shake this uncomfortable, nervous feeling that is coursing through every vein in my body. I go over my questions that I've prepared for the meeting with Susan Wilder, but I can't think of most of the answers I've rehearsed.

I finally pull up to the front of my dad's office building in downtown San Jose and find one of his golf shirts in the bag from the back seat. I put it over my head, mash my hair under one of his old baseball hats, and walk a few blocks to the closest pizza place. I buy a small pie and a large pie and shovel a piece from the large into my mouth as I walk quickly back to the building holding them on my shoulder like a delivery person. I bribe the security guard with the small pie and he points me to the elevator bank, which looks different in the light of day. No longer ominous to me, it almost looks ordinary. I confidently step in alongside a middle-aged man, who does not look up from his Blackberry.

Life rewards those who prepare, I think. *I'm finally going home.*

I turn around with the pizza resting on one arm, and as the doors come together, a sense of calm comes over me. The elevator starts moving up and my mind drifts back to Gavin for a moment. I'm not paying attention, and we come to a stop at the eighth floor. The doors open and I am frozen, looking over at the man who's now no longer next to me, adding to my shock. There's a woman in a navy-blue pantsuit and glasses who is waiting outside the doors, and at first I only see her side profile because she is deep in conversation on her mobile phone. As the doors open fully, she seems to recognize me, lowers the phone and smiles.

"Oh, wonderful! You got in! C'mon, the conference room is over here! Do I need to sign something? Smells delicious!"

She grabs the pizza from me, and I stumble forward trying to hold onto it, tripping over my feet, out of the elevator and onto the eighth floor. I whip back around as fast as I can, but it's too late. Suddenly it's silent and pitch black all around me.

18
YEAR 8

KENDALL

I stand in the darkness and begin to hear what sounds like the faint voice of a child. The voice is counting. For a second I think, *I'm dead, and I am on my way to heaven. This is it.*

Suddenly light pours in all over me, and I can't see.

"Found ya!"

When my eyes finally adjust to the light, I see a young boy with sandy blonde hair looking down at me. I look around and I am surrounded by coats and wrapping paper. I stare back at the little boy in shock.

"C'mon poop-face, get out of the closet! It's my turn to hide!" The boy reaches down and pulls me up by my right armpit. I look down at my knees and under the grass stains there's no scar.

I inspect my hands, so small and soft, and my socked feet. They are both so tiny I can't believe they are attached to my body.

"Start counting!" young Mike yells in a muffled voice from some unknown location.

A child's voice reverberates through my head as I begin, "One...two...three..."

I enter the kitchen, "four...five...six..."

The counter is twice as high as I remember and I can't see over it, "seven...eight...nine...ten...ready-or-not, here I come!"

I hear a faint giggle followed by a thump.

"Kendall and Michael! Time to get cleaned up for dinner!" my Mom calls from upstairs.

Mike pokes his little blonde head out of the recycling bin, knocking several plastic cartons onto the ground in the process, gives me a big grin, and runs up the stairs. I follow suit, using my hands to help me navigate them, in sort of an upwards scramble. The stairs seem freakishly tall in comparison to what I remember.

After I'm forced to take a bath and put on a dress for what my mom claims is a 'special dinner,' she sits behind me on my bed and brushes my damp, tangled hair back gently and carefully into a ponytail. The feeling of the brush against my scalp makes my entire body relax and allows my brain to stop trying to make sense of my surroundings. For a moment, I forget that I'm even further from my mind's age.

"All done. Now—do you want to bring Mr. Tickles with us, or should he stay home and rest?" She says with a genuine smile while holding up my ratty stuffed rabbit.

I reach out to touch Mr. Tickles and suddenly feel like I might cry. This is hopeless. I am a child, and children do not drive cars, or go to large office buildings alone, or convince adults that they are twenty years older than they actually are. I'm stuck here, and I'm going to have to go through puberty a second time.

"I want to bring him."

19

MIKE

Mom told me if I behave tonight at dinner we might get ice cream after. I don't get why she doesn't have a birthday cake. I love birthday cake. She said all she wanted was for Dad to take her to eat pizza where they met. Before Ken and I were born. I love pizza too, but I really don't want to take a bath and put on my scratchy shirt that she always makes me wear when we go out to places. I think I'll get chocolate ice cream.

I get my special seat in the van, all the way in the back, and Kendall sits in her booster seat in front of me. It's fun to poke her through the seat because she gets mad and then gets in trouble for yelling at me. I can't wait until tomorrow at school because me and Gavin have new Slammers, and we are gonna win everyone's Pogs.

The city is really big and really cool. The buildings are so tall it hurts my neck to look all the way to the top. Dad lets me ride on his back, and we point out all the fancy cars in the parking garage. On the street, there are so many different kinds of people. I hope the pizza place has crayons and one of those paper tablecloths so I can draw a T-Rex and a velociraptor.

20

KENDALL

While we wait for our pizza, Mike hoards all the crayons so I stir my Sprite with my straw. The restaurant is in a sad, dilapidated strip mall in an area of San Jose that's been later bulldozed and replaced by a Whole Foods or something. There are worn out brown vinyl booths around the perimeter of the inside, and in the middle, several old wooden tables with mismatched chairs. We sit at a table near the center of the restaurant, and I hold the giant laminated menu with low resolution photos of pasta and other generic Italian foods up in front of my face. We've already ordered, but I'm pretending to be engrossed in the menu anyway, trying not to talk too much because I don't remember what an eight-year-old has to say. So I just try to be a normal child and listen to my parents.

"I'm sorry I've been working so late this week," my dad says as he takes my mom's hand in his, "Happy belated birthday, Kath." They clink their plastic cups together, and my mom looks over at Mike and me.

"So did you guys know that Mommy and Daddy had their first date right at this very table?" my mom asks us.

Mike continues drawing and nods his head. My mom is smiling and looking down at me, waiting for my reply.

"At this table?" I ask in a high-pitched tone, trying to sound surprised. I've heard this story at least a thousand times.

"She was the most beautiful girl I'd ever seen," my dad says, looking at my mom, who then looks down at her hands, blushing.

Thankfully, the pizza arrives before the PDA can escalate. Mike practically jumps out of his seat with excitement, "I want pepperoni!"

I look at the massive pie, with its layers of sauce, cheese and pools of grease and my mouth starts to water. Then my inner-voice reminds me of how much saturated fat and calories are in one slice. I hesitate.

"Here, sweetie," my mom hands me a plate with a huge, beautiful, glistening slice of pizza.

Wait a second, I think, *I'm eight. I can eat whatever the hell I want and it doesn't matter. I have no one to impress.*

I devour the piece in no time and start on a second slice. My parents are deep in conversation with each other, and so they don't really notice as I grab for a third.

"Save room for ice cream, because we're going to your dad's favorite place!"

Mike rejoices at the sound of dessert and continues furiously scribbling on his kid's menu, pausing occasionally for a small bite of pizza or a sip of soda. My parents talk about work and church and other typical parent topics. I am bored and restless so I start to organize everyone's plates and napkins into neat piles for the waitress.

After making some good progress on our mess, my stomach begins its inevitable protest. A very loud gurgling sound emanates from beneath my shirt, and a wave of pain moves through my abdomen. No one else seems to notice, but the stabbing, blinding pain is my only focus. My mouth begins to salivate excessively and things get kind of hazy. I can feel my stomach churning around, and as my parents busy themselves calculating the tip, I jump out of my seat and run for the bathroom.

I don't quite make it.

21

MIKE

My mom yells at me to stop laughing and the waitress runs over with a bunch of towels and throws them at the ground beneath Kendall's feet. Kendall is standing in the middle of the restaurant with a pinkish red puddle in front of her. She is white like my dad's shirt.

My mom picks up Kendall, and they go to the girls' bathroom while my dad cleans up her puke. He doesn't seem mad like when I spilled my Gatorade all over the living room carpet. Oh man, I hope we can still get ice cream tonight. Kendall always ruins everything.

Me and Dad walk outside and stand on the sidewalk to wait for Mom and Kendall. There are so many lights that it's hard to remember that it's night time. Dad points up at the Big Dipper, and I stare at the moon until I have a white spot stuck in my eye. Then I start swinging around and around a pole and start to get dizzy. Dad tells me to stop and come back and tell him about the constellations.

Before we can find Ursa Major, Mom comes out and she's carrying Kendall. She makes a shushing sign for us to be quiet because Kendall's asleep on her chest, with her legs wrapped around Mom's waist and her arms around her neck. Kind of like the baby koalas we saw at the zoo.

"Dad. Dad! Are we still getting ice cream? Please!" I whisper, tugging on his elbow.

"Mikey, we need to get Kendall to bed. She's not feeling so good," he says quietly, putting his hand on my head.

I look up at him, trying to stop my voice from sounding all wobbly, "Okay..."

He looks at Mom and she nods.

Dad messes up my hair and tells me we can go somewhere special for dessert. I am so excited that I skip alongside him down the shiny sidewalk.

Dad's office building is the tallest building in the city. It's so big that I can't even see the sky when I'm standing right in front of it. Dad has a special badge, and he lets me hold it while we wait for the elevator. I pretend I'm at a very fancy hotel like Kevin in *Home Alone 2*.

Then we are all in the elevator. Inside its gold and mirrored like *Charlie and the Chocolate Factory*, and I hold onto the railing with my arms behind me and let my body hang forward while I count each floor as the numbers light up, all the way up to nineteen. Then: *Ding!* We stop. The 'ding' wakes up Kendall, and she looks around all scared. I laugh.

22

KENDALL

I smell lavender and baby powder, and I realize my mom is carrying me. I pull myself back from her softness and warmth, extending my arms to look at her, and she looks back at me with love and concern. She smooths my hair away from my face and asks me if I want to be put down and I shake my head because it just feels right at this point in time.

I'm a combination of embarrassment, fatigue, and confusion. This place is unfamiliar—full of desks, stacks of papers and ancient computers. Mom carries me over to a room full of small white tables and chairs, a microwave and a kitchenette. She lowers me slowly until my feet are flat on the linoleum floor, but I stay close to her. She reaches down to hold my hand and doesn't ask me to speak. My dad goes over to the freezer, pulls out an industrial sized carton of chocolate ice cream and sets it down on the table. Mike rushes over and takes a seat at the table, and he turns to me and smiles.

"C'mon, Kendall. Come sit next to me."

My mom smiles down at me, and I let go of her hand and run over to sit next to Mike. Mom sits across from us, and Dad comes over from the cabinet with four spoons. He hands each of us one and uses his own to scoop an enormous spoonful of ice cream straight out of the container and into his mouth. His cheeks puff out from the massive amount of sweet frozen cream, and a small amount dribbles out onto his chin. Mike and I both laugh and look at each other. My mom laughs and rolls her eyes.

Suddenly my dad drops his spoon and grabs the sides of his forehead, "Oh no!" he moans, "ice cream headache!"

Mike erupts in giggles, nearly falling out of his chair. He then takes his turn, diving spoon-first into the ice cream carton and taking an equally huge scoop. He can't even fit it in his mouth, and so half of the melted mass ends up smeared down his chin. I pick up my spoon and look at my mom, and she winks at me. We both reach with our spoons and get a small bit of ice cream on the edge to taste it.

"Mmmm," my mom licks her lips, "The perfect ending to a perfect birthday."

She hugs me from behind and kisses my hair, and for a split second, I feel like I could stay here forever. But the only certainty I have about this time in my life is that this feeling is transient, and things will never be this simple again.

As my dad cleans up our ice cream dribbles off the table, my feeling of belonging begins to dissipate. In its place is a sinking anxiety that my time is running out to get home. If I get taken back to my parents' house, there's no way I'll ever get back to the elevator. When you're a second-grader, adults don't just let you roam a city alone because you think you are a grown-up who traveled back in time. Nor will my parents be very jazzed about me ditching the whole family and escaping back into the elevator unaccompanied. The only idea I can come up with quickly is to manipulate Mike into helping me escape again. So I pop out of my chair in the break room and smack him on the back, "You're it!" and I sprint off towards the elevator bank.

I'm gone so fast my mom's voice calling out to us is just a blur of distant sound. I'm sure she's telling us to slow down and stay nearby, but I don't heed any of her potential warnings. I can hear Mike's heavy steps thumping louder and louder behind me until I'm confident he's right on my heels.

I make a sudden, sharp turn at the end of a row of cubicles and scramble to hide under a desk, as Mike goes whizzing by. I hear his steps slow a bit and stop at the end of the row.

"Michael Robert—" my mom's stern tone echoes across the large room. As she approaches, I take my final opportunity, and sprint towards the elevator. I push the button and wait, bouncing with adrenaline and looking back to make sure I'm a safe distance away. My brother's eyes circle the office and finally meet mine, as he sprints in my direction with a satisfied grin on his face. The doors open and I rush inside, hit the *28*, and pound the *CLOSE* button as many times as I can in rapid succession. My mom comes around the corner, spotting her eight-year-old daughter in an elevator alone and starts to run, remarkably fast, towards me.

"Kendall! No!" she waves her arms, still a few feet from the eighth-floor lobby.

I want to assure her that everything will be fine in a few seconds when the doors come together.

23

KENDALL

I stand in the quiet elevator and wait. Nothing happens. I push the number *28* button ten times in rapid succession, and there is no whirring or dinging or shifting. I fold my skinny arms and stare at the button, which is nearly at my eye-level, willing it to light up. After a number of silent, still minutes, panic starts to build inside me. Normally this would mean a steadily climbing pulse, the onset of shallow, rapid breathing and of course a completely rational feeling of impending doom. Instead I feel heavy, like gravity has an extra grip on my limbs. Exhausted, I sit cross-legged in the middle of the elevator, and my eight-year-old reflection looks back at me in the shiny elevator door. As I sit silently, a whisper of a thought begins growing larger in my mind, eventually building on itself until it's impossible to ignore—

What is my reality?

On the outside I look eight, but my mind is twenty-eight. All I have to prove my age are my memories and experiences. And most of my years have been spent looking to the next step.

Is reality the present? Or is reality just a concept in my mind?

Normally when my mind starts racing like this, sleep is the most desired outcome and the least likely possibility. But I guess an eight-year-old body needs sleep much more than a quarter-century one. In this dark, quiet elevator, my eyes become very heavy and my thoughts become a faint murmur in the back of my mind as I rest my head on my small hands. I linger somewhere between awake and asleep when a familiar sound enters my consciousness—

<DING>

24
YEAR 19

KENDALL

The room around me glows orange with the early morning light flooding through the uncurtained windows. Laying on my stomach, I feel a layer of softness and warmth underneath me and a light blanket across my back. Pushing up onto my elbows, I realize I am in a bed. There's a faint sound of snoring next to me, and suddenly I feel the mass of a human body roll over towards me. Instinctively I jump, my momentum knocking me to the floor in a heap.

Luckily the loud thump does not seem to wake my bedmate. Looking down at myself, I am wearing only an old T-shirt and underwear. Feeling suddenly very exposed, I crawl around on the floor, desperate for somewhere to hide. As I lean up against the bedside table, I pull the bottom hem of the T-shirt around my knees, covering my bare legs, and I scan the room for something to defend myself with. Or any evidence of my clothes or belongings.

My surroundings are strangely familiar, almost like I find myself back in a recurring dream. The room around me is neat and uncluttered, but clearly masculine, with navy blue and tan bedding and blown-up black-and-white posters of Einstein and Marilyn Monroe. The latter poster triggers a memory of a public argument— my side of the debate was that Marilyn Monroe was not really that traditionally beautiful, but her sex appeal and femininity made up for her lack of symmetry. Chris, my boyfriend at the time, adamantly disagreed. His stance was that hot and beautiful were one and the same. Laced with too many martinis, we ended up getting so pissed at each other that I stormed off and walked home to his apartment in StuyTown by myself. Reflecting back to this time in my life, this embarrassingly public display likely stemmed from my own physical inadequacy in the context of our mainly superficial relationship. I was never going to be the hot girl, so I wasn't Chris's ideal. And I am now in that very apartment where I cried myself to sleep that night, longing to be enough for him.

Chris rolls over again and groans. His glasses sit above me on the bedside table, resting on top of his Organic Chemistry textbook. I have lost track of what day of the week it is. *Friday? Saturday? Do I let him wake up and find me here? Or do I just leave and end things now?*

"Good morning," Chris says sleepily. I look up at him and he's smiling at me with a curious look in his blue eyes, "What are you doing on the floor?"

It's too late for me to make an escape, and I'm tired and literally unable to think on my feet. Or knees, rather.

"I'm, um, lost," I say.

He laughs into his pillow, grabbing my wrist and yanking me back up into bed and on top of him. His smell is familiar and makes my cheeks warm. I'm reminded of our physical attraction, and the good memories that I've stuffed away for so long inevitably follow it. He nuzzles his chin into my neck and breathes, "Not yet."

I start to relax into him initially but when my better judgment creeps back into my consciousness, I start to hesitate and arch backwards awkwardly. It's been at least seven years since I've seen him, and I don't like this power he still seems to have over me. He grins, thinking I'm playing some kind of flirtatious game, and grabs the back of my head, pulling me towards him and kissing me slowly and deeply. I feel him harden against me, and our kissing becomes more feverish and desperate. Some part of me that I forgot existed catches on fire, and the fire expands from my core out to every edge of my skin. I find myself unable to put a coherent thought together, so I just react to his touch, pushing my body closer and closer to his. And for the first time in four days, I forget about rushing back to my twenty-eight-year-old life.

25

MIKE

It's a beautiful morning for a lacrosse game. The air is cool and dry, like most mornings in Boulder, but the sun is warming the bench where I sit gearing up for the scrimmage. I normally wake up with a ton of meaningless thoughts running through my head, but on game days my mental energy is completely focused on the win. It's like my mind is a tunnel and the only outlet is the back of the net. It's a fantastic feeling.

I know there's a crowd behind me, my parents are here in the stands somewhere, and my teammates are next to me, but I am mentally alone.

As the warning horn blares, I put in my mouthguard and shove my helmet over my head. I jump a few times to loosen my legs and shake out some of the adrenaline that's coursing through my body. I approach my opponent for the face-off and the ref puts the ball between our sticks as we crouch to the ground. We are nothing but pure energy, waiting for our release. The whistle blows and we wrestle our sticks over the ball with all of our might. I know without a doubt that I will be the victor, as I shoulder my opponent out of the way and scoop the ball into a pass back to my long stick behind me. I sprint down towards the goal, with my heart pounding in my ears, and he passes it up to me on the fly as I cut towards the goal. I'm on a fast-break and the goalie is my last obstacle. All in less than half a second, I cut sideways in front of him, and cradle around to confuse him. I shift my weight back to the direction I came from, and suddenly there is a loud pop. My mind doesn't register why I'm falling to the ground until the blinding pain starts. I realize the crowd, that was just a blurred roar in the back of my consciousness, is now silent.

KENDALL

I sip my green tea and watch the people walking by our favorite breakfast place. In my mind's timeline, I haven't been here in a long time, and I now remember why we loved this place so much. The tea has the perfect level of sweetness, the croissants are warm and fresh, and the people coming and going are interesting and diverse. Only in the Village will you see a man with a Mohawk and skateboard alongside a well-dressed woman in a hijab, with a glamorous yet subdued air of sophistication.

The uncomfortable tension I felt earlier with Chris is muted now that he's acting very content and casual. He makes conversation about his 'idiot' microbiology lab TA, and as he speaks, I assess that we probably haven't been dating very long at this point since he takes the time to listen to my responses and makes excuses to touch me throughout the morning. His blue eyes also hold my gaze without drifting around the cafe for other, more interesting people.

After breakfast, we walk by the brownstones on the lower east side holding hands and he talks about our future. I am so comfortable that I don't immediately notice the irony in this.

"After I finish my residency at Columbia, and I open my practice, I'll buy you this one," he nods towards the corner brownstone with flower boxes in the windows and marble steps. It's so immaculate that I imagine photos of it likely already grace the pages of several noteworthy design magazines. I remain quiet and simply smile, not wanting to interrupt the game.

"I'll buy an old Ferrari like the one in *Ferris Bueller's Day Off*," he pauses, "and we can cruise over to our summer home on Martha's Vineyard for long weekends."

He looks at me deviously and pokes my stomach, "And we can get you a boob job."

I hit him playfully on the arm, trying not to act as offended as I am by that comment that used to be commonplace in our relationship. He laughs, picks me up over his shoulder, and runs down the street. I scream and hit him again hard on the butt. I remember this day now. It was one of our best.

As we approach his gentrified ten-story building on the east side of the city, I'm not sure if I can continue this day as I remember it without having to relive the later pain.

But maybe, the delusional part of my mind interjects, *if I really try to make him happy this time, I won't have to.*

Nine years ago, after breakfast, we went back to his apartment, talking and laughing and flirting, and made love on the couch with *Grey's Anatomy* on in the background. Then I read his case studies to him, while we laid there intertwined, and quizzed him on his diagnoses. We finally got dressed about six hours later and met his pre-med friends out at their usual wine bar.

We step into the lobby just like we did all those years ago, and this time I watch him closely. He's extremely handsome, just like I remember but constantly try to forget. His normally parted and smooth sandy brown hair is messy, and his rare, small amount of stubble emphasizes his chiseled jaw. He is fair, but not pale, and his eyes are crystal blue. He's not a large guy but is a few inches taller than me and very lean and athletic. He holds my hand with his right hand and fiddles with his Blackberry with his left.

A small Asian woman with a metal rolling cart full of brown paper bags shuffles up to outside of the lobby entrance shortly after us, and as we wait for the elevator, she barely manages to open the heavy door and then has very little success in maneuvering her grocery cart through it. Realizing that Chris is completely oblivious to her struggles, I rush over to hold it open for her and she grumbles at me as if I'm causing her more delay rather than assistance, waving me out of her way. As the elevator we were waiting for opens, my Asian friend rushes into the elevator, blocking our path, and the doors close quickly between us before we can protest.

We exit the stairwell on the fourth floor, panting from the sudden exertion, and after a few steps down the hall, Chris's eyes and thumb return to his Blackberry.

"Candace said she and John are going to meet us at Sloane's later."

Sloane's is the wine bar we always went to, and Candace is his classmate that he started fucking a week after we broke up.

About two years from now, I estimate in my head.

My face flushes with anger at this thought. As we approach the door to his apartment, our breathing finally returning to normal, he reaches towards my face and kisses me again. This time my mind is not empty but conflicted.

Maybe I can have a new version of today. Maybe the future will be slightly altered, but still the version that aligns with my life goals. Maybe I gave up too quickly on us.

I might be delusional but I also finally feel...wanted.

He pulls back, smiling at me and unlocks the door. We enter the apartment, and I stand awkwardly near the entrance, considering what impact my sudden disappearance might have on my future. But my legs are frozen in place and my brain is clouded by good memories. He takes off his coat, hanging it carefully on a wooden hanger in the front closet, and lines up his keys, wallet and Blackberry in their spot on a shelf by the small, modern kitchen. He grabs the remote from its basket on the coffee table and turns on the TV. He doesn't say word but pulls me towards him, kissing me intensely and taking off my shirt in one quick motion, laying me back on the stiff couch. The sad, melodramatic music from *Grey's* plays over the episode-concluding montage, and I stop and pull back from Chris. He looks at me with a hopeful desire and I reach for the remote and change the channel. He unbuttons my jeans as I hear the faint murmur of Bob Ross painting his happy clouds.

I can hear my phone ringing in my purse but I ignore it and pull his polo up over his head.

26

MIKE

My dad wheels me out to the covered drop-off area outside the emergency room, and the giant ice pack on my knee burns.

"Stay here Kath, I'll pull the car around."

My mom doesn't respond audibly to my dad but I know she's behind me nodding. As crazy as my mom can be about God and religion, and how irritating she can be about her unrealistic standards and expectations for her children, I will hand it to her, she does know how important silence is sometimes. After four hours in the ER, I do not want to speak or be spoken to. My pain pills are making me sleepy but they do nothing to numb the anger and disappointment. I wonder if this all might just be a dream, or, rather, a nightmare. The dull ache in my knee reminds me it's an unfortunate reality.

My parents are staying at a hotel nearby, and so they drop me off at home. They announce that they are going to let me rest and they'll be back later to get me for dinner.

"I don't feel like going to dinner anymore," I say with my eyes closed, resting my head back against the metal pole of the wheelchair to keep the room from spinning. I don't know how anyone gets hooked on Oxycontin—I just feel like someone put me in a fucking blender on liquefy.

"Okay, honey. Well, we can just bring some food in for you and Gavin then," my mom says, her voice several octaves higher than normal. Like if her tone is perky enough then maybe I'll forget that my life is over.

I'm sure Gavin's probably on his way back from the mountain. He'll usually go to my games in the morning and then hit up the slopes for a few runs before it's time to start drinking again. He tried to go with my parents to the ER, my mom said, but I told her not to let him.

After a series of awkward shifts from the wheelchair to the car, car to the door to my apartment, and then onto the living room couch, I can tell my dad is exhausted as he wipes beads of sweat from his forehead. My mom fusses around, giving me pillows and water and hopelessly trying to clean a trail through the shitshow of our apartment.

They finally leave, after one hundred reassurances that they can return instantly if I even so much as fart wrong, and I fall asleep for what feels like days. I awaken in the dim light of dusk, and it's quiet, so I assume I'm still alone. But then I hear a familiar slurping and chomping coming from the kitchen.

Him and his fucking Lucky Charms.

I start to try and sit up and I knock over the glass of water on the coffee table with my good knee, "Fuck!"

"Well, hello there," Gavin says with half a mouth-full of milk and cereal, "how was your nap?" he grins.

"Shut the fuck up and get me some paper towels," I bark.

"Well, didn't somebody wake up on the wrong side of the shitty 1980s pull-out couch?" he says in his mocking tone.

He comes over and drops a wad of paper towels on the spill and presses his foot over them, leaving them stuck to the carpet in the form of a water footprint.

"So you got the good stuff, huh?" he motions towards the prescription bottle.

"Yea, it fucking hurts still though. They said I'm gonna need surgery but they have to wait a few days."

"I'm really sorry, man. That's really shitty."

He stands over me, turning to look out the living room window. I just close my eyes and lean back. We are both silent for several minutes.

He sits down on the papasan chair across the room from me and turns on the TV.

"Wanna play some Mariokart?"

I open my eyes and he's holding a controller out towards me. I stare blankly at the controller.

"Fine. I get Toad though," I smile weakly.

27

KENDALL

I stand in a towel and look at my reflection in the foggy mirror in Chris's bathroom. My wet hair looks even darker than the golden brown I am starting to become accustomed to seeing in each reflection. I clear a section of the mirror off with my hand so that I can put on my makeup, and pause, staring at myself. My face is slightly tanned from my daily walk to and from campus, and a few freckles are popping out on my nose and cheeks. My green eyes have no lines around them, and there's still a little baby fat under my cheek bones, but I look about the same as I did in the gas station two 'days' ago. I decide I actually don't hate my hair long like this and this strange thought triggers a more concerning one—I haven't blogged in five days, and I've never missed more than a day since I moved to New York.

I happened upon food blogging right at the perfect time, before it exploded into every amateur housewife's part-time hobby. I started as a way to build my extracurricular portfolio for my law school application, and then I found myself writing posts every weekend rather than cracking open my LSAT practice book. But the desire to capture my every meal with well-lit and well-thought out digital photos, as well as clever prose about the history of the food and unique blends of ingredients was more well-received than I could have ever imagined. My followers wanted more and more quirky cafes and more interesting things to do with coconut milk, and I loved their enthusiasm about my calorie counts and new ways to reinvent pesto. So against my parents' and my boyfriend's advice, I dove headfirst into the food blogging world. I deferred my acceptance into Fordham, and my mom gave me the silent treatment. Which I perpetuated for months, happily. Blogging gave me instant gratification in the form of approval and acceptance that I had never experienced before, and companies wanted to pay me for ad space and guest appearances. So I didn't need my parents' monthly stipend and daily guilt-trips anymore. And, the bottom line is, I can't afford to slow down my posts this early in my career path and lose any followers. I need to find a computer.

Brushing my hair back away from my face, my green eyes stare back at me, and for a second I feel like I recognize something in them. Then there's a knock on the bathroom door.

"You alive in there?" Chris calls.

I'm not sure, I think.

Calling out that I'll be out in a minute, I shake my head to rid myself of this strange feeling. I decide I'll just write a quick post about Sloane's after we get back tonight. I just need to make sure not to have too much wine—buzzed writing quickly becomes the ramblings of a sixteen-year-old fangirl.

I finish my makeup and shove a small notepad and pen into my clutch. Chris calls out for me to hurry up, and we hold hands again for the three-block walk to the open-air wine bar. For once, it's actually nice to have someone to share the air with. He talks about MCATs and the glowing review his professor gave his term paper. I start to daydream like I did as a kid and tune him out inadvertently as we walk. I imagine that I'm standing in front of a large audience, at some kind of book store, reading a writing passage and random people come out of the shelves of books surrounding us and start interrupting my reading. Instead of stopping, I continue reading, my voice growing louder and louder until I am screaming the words in front of me.

"Kendall?" Chris says as we approach Sloane's, "You didn't answer me."

"Oh, I'm sorry, Chris," I say, embarrassed of my uncharacteristically wandering mind, "Yes, I agree."

"Awesome. I'm so glad," he smiles as he turns away and enters the wine bar.

I have no idea what I agree with.

Chris lights up when he's around John and Candace, which I probably should have noticed all those years ago. He talks and talks about their courses and med school interviews next year, and I just spin my wine glass and smile on the rare occasion that anyone makes eye contact with me. I realize for the first time that Chris is kind of boring. And self-obsessed. After about a half hour of this, the attention unfortunately turns to me.

"So Kendall, Chris said you are a blogger—I've never really heard of that. Is it like a chat room, or message board-thing?" Candace asks me, with genuine interest.

What a bitch.

"Well, not really," they all look at my expectantly, so I continue, "I'm like a food and restaurant critic combined with a chef, kind of like the guy who writes for the *Sunday Times*, but it's all online for my readers. I take digital pictures of the food I make after testing out different recipes, and I also have a daily write-up about the next up-and-coming trends in the food industry."

"Oh really?" she pauses, dipping a piece of bread in the olive oil dish, "So like, what do you want to do when you graduate? As a career?"

"Um...blogging can be pretty lucrative. I'm trying get sponsored by online magazines and manufacturing companies and stuff."

The three are silent. Soon-to-be doctors are very uncomfortable with hypotheticals.

"That's cool—sounds interesting!" John adds enthusiastically to break the silence.

Chris, of course, jumps at the opportunity to talk about himself, "As future physicians, I think we can learn a lot from food and nutrition science. Modern medicine is extremely important, but if our patients don't understand that unhealthy food leads to obesity and cardiac disease, we can't really impact their lives by just putting a superficial bandage on the problem with statins and betablockers."

This sparks a new topic of debate for the three, about their recent experiences in their pharmacology lecture, and I excuse myself to go to the bathroom. I stand in the stall and scribble notes on my notepad about the topic of tonight's blog—*wine and cheese accompaniment.* I try to stay on topic, but suddenly I find myself writing about Chris jumping up and clearing the wine off the table in one-fell swoop, grabbing Candace, and shoving his tongue down her throat as they proceed to get it on in front of John and I. Someone opens the bathroom door and my attention shifts back to reality.

My mind is playing tricks on me.

I close my notepad, freshen up my makeup, and head back to the table. As I walk through the small, crowded restaurant, my phone suddenly starts ringing. I look down to see who is calling, then back at my boyfriend and his enthusiastic conversation across the room. I think about chocolate ice cream and lavender. For the first time in what feels like eons, I go against my better judgment and decide to answer the call.

"Hey, Mom."

28

MIKE

Now that my chances of competing at the pro level of lacrosse are non-existent, and my knee is preventing me from snowboarding with Gavin, I have re-discovered my love of getting high. Boulder is a great place to find pot too—you can even have it delivered to your house.

A few days out from my surgery and I could give a fuck about lacrosse. All I want to do is sit here and smoke and eat Cheez-Its and watch the *Lord of the Rings* trilogy. Most days, Gavin will join me for a morning smoke session, but then he has to go to class, or work, and probably goes snowboarding after. He doesn't tell me that he does, because he doesn't want to rub it in, but I can tell when the carpet's damp from his snowboarding boots.

"Dude, wake up," Gavin says as he kicks the bottom of my shoe fairly hard, "There's an imprint of your ass in this couch and it's losing its luxurious softness."

"Fuck, man! I'm tired alright?"

"Smoking and sleeping really taking it out of ya, huh?"

"What the fuck do you care? You smoke every day."

"Look man, I know I love pot, but I also like a little human and nature interaction once in a while. Feeds the soul."

"Oh, fuck off with that hippie shit."

"I'm serious. C'mon, we're going out."

"No. I'm comfortable."

Growing up Gavin was always smaller than me. Actually, I guess after freshman year of high school, he had me height-wise by about three inches or so, but a strong wind could have blown the guy over. He was nothing but a skinny little punk, and I used it to my advantage by outrunning him or whooping his ass as needed. But after the last few years of snowboarding and stocking shelves at PriceMart, he has become enormous. He grabs me under my arms and throws me like a small child from the couch into the papasan chair.

"Watch it, dick! My knee!"

He ignores me and grabs the couch cushions and all the pillows and throws them out the front door into the snow.

"Time to go. It's not comfortable here anymore anyway."

I look up at him, shocked and appalled.

He hands me my crutches and holds the door open for me. He is not normally one to tell anyone what to do. I am too high and tired to try and fight him, so I follow him out of the apartment.

29

KENDALL

I talked to my mom that night for close to an hour. She told me about my dad's upcoming retirement, about how she started a part-time job at the library in town, and of course about Mike's injury. To be honest, I don't think we've talked for more than five minutes at a time since I left for NYU. Our conversation was not without its awkward pauses and resentful undertones, and it's not like our relationship was suddenly back on track, but as soon as the call was over I felt an odd sense of relief wash over me.

After I got off the phone, I realized I had been sitting on the curb outside of Sloane's for over an hour, and Chris had not once come out to inquire about my whereabouts. So for the first time in forever, I didn't hesitate. I walked into the restaurant, up to the table, and announced to Chris that our relationship just wasn't working for me. That I really had to focus on my career. Exactly what he would tell me one year and ten months later when he left for medical school in Boston. The best part was I think I saw Candace's jaw hit the floor when I said it.

I then went back to my apartment, where my roommate probably had forgotten what I looked like, and locked myself in my room. And I just started writing. Not about grilled chicken, creme brulee, or goat cheese. Not about the best Soho cafe to take your girlfriends. I wrote about real life first, then it evolved into the opposite. I wrote a stream of consciousness tale of going back in time and starting over and that evolved into fictitious creatures that were outside of time looking in at me. It was complete crap, but I loved every second of it. I felt...free.

Two days passed, and I called my mom three times. I got an update on my grandmother, and how our house was slowly falling apart, and then got an in-depth report on my mom's disagreement with their couple-friends at church. I was not that interested in any of it, but the more I listened, the more I realized what she was trying to say—she just needed to be heard.

I'm not sure what my parents did when my brother told them I had unprotected sex and potentially an early term abortion. But I know what they didn't do. They didn't ask me how or why, or if I said no. They couldn't see past their own small-minded religiosity to even ask if I was okay. I was now a problem to be dealt with, first with silent punishment and then with overwhelming guilt.

We just don't know where we went wrong, my mother cried to me, as I threw as many items in a bag as I could, red-faced and clenching my jaw.

With everything! I screamed at her, and then in between sobs I told them I was never coming home again, and I meant it.

My dad didn't say much, but I saw in his eyes that he was hopeless about my future. It was like all my accomplishments in life were now completely obscured by this one night. And my parents, who taught me to never give up, were giving up on me.

As I hang up the phone with my mom, my face flushes with this memory—partially with regret and mostly with anger. I doubted her love for me for so long, or at least I felt that it was conditional. And maybe it was to a small extent, but now that she's a real person to me, with her own insecurities and doubts and mistakes, I can't really hate her for that anymore. Because the one thing that this journey has taught me is that everything in time and in life is conditional.

I'm nineteen today, and so the night with the Asshole will not happen for two more years. If this year is before the alternate experience, maybe it won't happen at all. Maybe I can stop it from ever starting.

So after I freed my mind of this anger and resentment, I had mental space for new things. And I just started writing. I wrote, and wrote, and wrote. I wrote about knights and medieval maidens. I wrote about Sunnyvale and about faraway places. I wrote about a daughter, and about a mother. I wrote about a brother.

The more I wrote Mike in my characters, the more I remembered how much I needed him. He carried me home when I thought I broke my ankle roller-blading. He defended me when the entire school circulated with rumors about yet-to-be-determined sexual preferences. He let me tag along with him when I was an annoying teenager who claimed I was twenty-eight years old. I missed my brother.

So that's why I'm sitting here at the dinky Boulder airport, after taking two long connections to get here, and waiting for a taxi. To kill some time, I'm working on a new piece, and I have no idea where it's going nor do I know if anyone will ever even read it. Regardless, I can't help but scribble down some cool images from the taxi ride.

> *Endless trees, natural complexities in the landscape, crisp mountain air, a mile-high world whizzing by my window.*

Even the sun here feels different than in Manhattan. It makes things look more alive.

—

The taxi pulls up to the address that my mom gave me, and I take a deep breath and walk up to the door. It's dusk, but there is still enough light to see the gorgeous mountains in the distance. I knock on the door and wait, my heart in my throat. I knock again.

There is silence on the other end of the door, indicating that there's clearly no one home to answer. I look at my cell phone and it's seven PM. To me, since I've been traveling across time zones, on top of jumping around them, the lack of familiarity and hopelessness of this moment weighs on every inch of me, and I am just utterly exhausted. I jiggle the doorknob out of desperation, and it's locked. I consider calling my mom to get Mike's phone number but I decide I will just wait a little while before I worry her. I collapse on the front stoop in a heap and to distract myself from my anxiety I continue moving my pen until I lose track of the words on the page.

30

MIKE

Gavin and I get out of the truck and sit on the back of his bumper. He opens a beer with his keychain, takes a swig, and passes the bottle to me silently as the sun sets over the lake below us.

"I come up here a lot just to get out of my own head," Gavin says, looking out at the glassy water.

I don't say anything but just watch the sky. I take a big swig of the beer.

"Look, man. I know this is a completely shitty situation, but you can't just give up on life because you can't play."

I clench my jaw. I can't even find words to express how angry I am, so I take the beer bottle and chuck it as hard as I can at a big rock. It shatters loudly, the rock and the ground surrounding it now glittering with the brown shards. I regret the decision immediately, because now there's no more beer to numb my anger.

We don't speak again until the sun is just a faint glow over the edge of the water. Gavin is the first to break the silence.

"My mom's sick. It's not good," he looks down at his hands.

"What?"

"Cancer. Fucking cigarettes."

"Dude, I—when did you find out?"

"About a week ago. My dad called me—said he's gotta make some arrangements—needs me to come back to Sunnyvale to help."

"Arrangements?"

"We've gotta sell the Tahoe. Money's tight and chemo's not cheap apparently. And other shit like move some furniture around and make calls."

"Shit, man."

"Yea."

In the dim light of dusk, Gavin's face appears to have aged since we sat down. He rubs the space between his eyes, and I can tell that his mind is off running somewhere else entirely. I've known this man since we could barely spell our own names, and he is eternally optimistic.

When we were five, he was convinced that he could swim despite having never received one lesson. Gavin just had no reservations about literally diving in. When adult swim was over that day, he went up on the diving board and jumped off, sinking straight to the bottom. Luckily the lifeguard on duty was actually paying attention, and he was pulled out after a few seconds. You think that discouraged him from getting up there again? Gavin had to be chaperoned at all times the rest of the summer because he would try to sneak back over to make another plunge. People thought he might be mentally challenged or that he was a born adrenaline-junkie with no common sense. But Gavin just didn't understand why everyone was so freaked out because he knew he'd be fine. He was *Gavin*. In his mind, of course he would eventually get the hang of the swimming thing.

Even through high school, he would continuously hit on the most gorgeous and popular girls and have no concept of embarrassment when they shut him down. This overconfidence started to pay off for him once we moved to Boulder, as for some reason college girls were drawn to his idiotic face. Probably because he was so damn big and so damn engaging. His size made him immediately stand out in a crowd, and then when you talked to Gavin, you felt like what you said really, truly mattered. Even if it was the half-baked ramblings of an eighteen-year-old with absolutely no worldly experience. He also smiled excessively, making him stand out everywhere since everyone else in Boulder was trying so hard to look unimpressed in that 'too-cool-for-this-spot' vibe. So he would clean up almost every night of the week, bringing nines and tens home to his dirty bedroom, while I generally went home with the less-attractive and more insecure sidekicks. The other nights, when we both came back empty-handed, Gavin was still completely convinced that it went the best that it could have—that it was their loss, as simple-minded Colorado girls. He would talk about the quality of girls back in northern California, how they were hotter and more interesting and then we'd slam some more beers and take turns punching holes in the bathroom wall. More than anything, he was just certain everything would work out. And I think I relied on that positivity more than I realized, because it suddenly felt like the world was literally falling apart at the shitty poncho seams.

"I don't think she has long," he says earnestly, looking at the sky.

I am speechless. There are things I want to say, but in this moment, pity seems like a cheap escape from the truth.

31

KENDALL

The sound of car tires on gravel wakes me, and I'm absolutely freezing. I hear one car door slam followed by a second. It's now pitch black, and I'm half-awake and fully confused. It takes me more than a moment to recall where I am. And then, how old I am. I curl into a ball and sit on my hands to try and warm them up. It's a different kind of cold than New York—it's incredibly still and dry, like the air is empty around me. I consider standing up and pulling out my phone to call my mom, and suddenly a huge heavy boot sounds like it stomps on the concrete directly in front of my face. I scream.

"Holy shit!" a man's voice yells and all in the same instant I hear him tumble sideways and into what sounds like a bush.

"What the hell?" another male voice yells from several yards back, "You alright?"

"It's okay!" I stand and yell at them, waving my arms as if they can see me surrendering "I'm just waiting for someone—I didn't mean to scare you!" My voice trails off at the end.

A light shines on my face and I'm blinded.

"What the he—Kendall?" My brother points the light from his keychain in the air so that I can see his face faintly and he's leaning on a pair of crutches, his knee in a large brace. His hair is much shorter since I saw him last, and he's put on some muscle. Well—before I was fifteen again—last time I saw him was probably when he came home the summer after his freshman year of college, before I left for NYU.

Without a thought, I run up to Mike and wrap my arms around him, crutches and all. He's stiff and unprepared for the hug. I feel the weight of the metaphorical space between us as I pull back and try to find the words to explain why I am sitting in the dark in front of his door after all this time.

"What the hell are you doing here?" he asks, and in the darkness I'm unsure if his tone is disappointed or angry or just surprised. Before I can respond, he moves towards the door of their apartment, "It's cold out here, let's go inside."

A light is switched on inside the door, and my eyes instinctively close from the sudden brightness. I blink them back to normalcy. The apartment is very small and dark; the walls covered with old wood paneling. There are only a few pieces of old ratty furniture, and I recognize most of them from my grandma's old house. Her overstuffed gray and pink sofa with the dust ruffle on the bottom sits against the wall with several old blankets scattered around it, across from that a papasan chair with a cushion that may have been cream-colored at some point but is now closer to a shade of tan, and then a wooden coffee table with an impressive number of old water rings. There are typical guy posters on the walls—pretty girls in bikinis that were most likely free with a case of beer—and then there is a pile of snowboarding gear in the corner. Mike leans on his crutches and gets a beer from the fridge. I stand in in the middle of the entryway and hug my arms tightly around my torso to keep them from shaking. I've started warming up slightly, but my fingers and toes are still numb and tingly. I breathe hot air into my right fist, and when I look up, a familiar face stands in the doorway to the kitchen, leaning next to the light switch. Seems like I can't escape him lately.

Gavin breaks the silence by laughing, "Fuckin-A, I've never been that scared in my life!"

He jumps a little and shakes imaginary cobwebs from his arms and legs. He looks at me with a huge smile, "How the heck are ya, Kendall?"

In two steps he crosses the small living room and puts his huge arms around me in a friendly embrace. I have that pain in the pit of my stomach again, and I want to pull back immediately, but he's so warm that I just stay still. I remind myself that our fight in Sunnydale hasn't happened yet, and I tense up a little more thinking about it.

He pulls back, not noticing my hesitation, "Geezus you're cold. Lemme get you a hoodie." Gavin disappears down the back hallway, and Mike stands in front of the door we just entered, leaning on his crutches again.

So I'm finally here, and even though I saw my brother a few days ago, the mood is completely different and his response is even more unpredictable. I try to choose my words carefully.

"Mom told me about your knee," I say timidly.

Mike finally looks up at me, "What are you doing here? Are you lost or something?"

"I came to see you."

"For what?"

"For—to be with my brother. Mom said you may need...help."

Gavin walks back over towards us and hands me a giant hooded sweatshirt with *UCB* in big letters on the front. I quickly pull it over my head and mutter a quiet thank you to him. I can feel him staring at me.

"I haven't talked to you in three years and I blow out my knee and suddenly you give a shit? How nice," he hops over to the couch and lays his crutches against the wall, sitting down slowly.

Gavin straightens, realizing a little late that he walked into a room of extreme awkwardness. His eyes meet mine and his anxiety is palpable.

"Mike, I—I'm sorry," I offer.

He turns on the TV and doesn't look at me. His jaw is set. "Sorry for what?"

"For being M.I.A. for all these years. I don't know—"

"It's whatever," he still does not look up.

"I'm really sorry. I never knew this happened to you. I always thought you quit lacrosse."

He finally looks me in the eye, with anger brimming behind his gaze, "why would I quit lacrosse Kendall?"

"I didn't—don't know. I just assumed—I'm sorry."

He takes a deep breath through set teeth and turns back to the TV.

"Stop apologizing. Just freaking sit down and relax for once in your life. You're stressing me out."

I follow his order and sit uncomfortably perched on the old papasan chair. Gavin pulls a chair from the kitchen table and sets it next to the couch where he sits facing the TV. Mike turns up SportsCenter, and we all just stare at the screen.

After a while, I'm finally thawing out, and a million thoughts are running through my head as I pretend to watch ESPN. Mainly they are thoughts of guilt and regret, but then they evolve into shock that my brother seems to actually care about not seeing me for a long period of time. In the past ten years, I never once thought he gave a shit about me. If I was wrong about that, I might have been wrong about his intentions when he was twenty-three and betrayed me to my parents. I guess since that hasn't happened yet his intentions don't really matter at this moment in time. They might have evolved over the years after my absence.

Then, my thoughts shift to how angry I made Gavin last time I saw him. When I glance in his direction, I catch him staring at me again. He looks away quickly and back at the TV and takes a drink of his Gatorade. I find myself watching his Adam's apple flex and move as he swallows the neon blue liquid, then wipes his tan forearm over his lips. He has grown up into a very attractive guy, with dark stubble lining his strong jaw and his brown hair naturally tousled on his head. He wears a T-shirt that's starting to fray a bit on the collar and edges of the sleeves, and over-sized gray sweatpants that seem to fall in the right place on his hips. My face flushes at this thought that I can't believe I'm having, so I shift my eyes over to Mike, and he's fallen asleep, half sitting up with his elbow on the arm of the couch and his head leaning in the crook of his arm. He doesn't snore, but his mouth hangs open in a heavy mouth-breathe slumber, like he fell asleep mid-sentence. My eyes are also getting heavy, and I decide I should at least attempt to brush my teeth before succumbing to my exhaustion.

In their bathroom that probably hasn't been cleaned in months, if ever, I lift up dirty towels and T-shirts in search of a tube of toothpaste. I find a small, nearly empty tube in a drawer that's mostly full of old razors, various types of condoms, and magazines.

As I splash warm water on my face, I think about my life in Manhattan—my so-called 'present' life, which is a stark contrast to my brother's here. My studio apartment is never less than immaculate, with the only clutter confined to an idea board that's littered with cut-outs of food and kitchen products (organized alphabetically of course). I think about Susan Wilder and then about my color-coordinated closet. And how I've been able to cut out the messiness of the world to keep my life on track.

I am already fairly successful, at least in the blogging world. I have a ton of followers of my food blog. They are loyal, always commenting on a new recipe with enthusiasm and support. They love me—at least it seems like they do.

But, then, I think, *who do they love?*

I mean, they can count every calorie in my breakfast, but do they know that when I get sad I just want to be alone with a pen and paper and silence? And that when I'm excited I can't help but do a ridiculous dance?

Does anyone really know me?

A knock on the bathroom door startles me, and I reach for the handle and ease the door open. Gavin stands in the dark hallway looking down at me with an odd look in his eyes—like he's seeing me for the first time. I guess, to him, at this point in time, he hasn't really seen me since they left for Boulder and since I grew up a little.

"I thought you might need a towel," he says as he looks down at my wet hands and holds the towel out for me to take. I rub my hands nervously over the rough cotton and put it up to my face, dabbing it dry.

"You can sleep in my bed tonight," he pauses, sliding his hands down the edge of the door to pull it back towards him, "I'll take the couch."

Normally I would inquire about the cleanliness of his sheets and the availability of a down pillow, but I'm distracted by the dark brown color of his eyes and can't look away, "Thanks."

He smiles at me with that lightness of his and my whole body seems to tingle. He turns to walk away, and I can't help but whisper after him.

"Gavin!"

He turns back around, and I walk into the hallway, now standing directly in front of him. He moves closer so that we are almost touching and leans down to make sure he can hear me. My mouth is within centimeters of his jaw and ear, and he smells like earth and soap and something unfamiliar that I never want to stop smelling. I can feel my heartbeat in my throat as I hold my breath. I finally whisper, "Thank you, for always being there. For Mike..." I trail off, embarrassed at my sudden onset of emotions.

He doesn't say anything but with a look I can't decipher I feel like his eyes laugh at me. I turn red and immediately regret trying to talk to this twenty-one-year-old guy about feelings.

I quickly move past him towards the bedroom, and I can feel his eyes follow me the whole way. I don't give him the chance to speak, as I ease the door closed and lean against it. I stand with my back against the door and it's like I can feel him in the space of the hallway, until I hear his footsteps trailing away from me. As if he were a magnetic force holding me against it, I am now able to be released by the distance between us. I crawl into his bed and lay there with that strange smell again, and I hug his pillow as I fight sleep thinking about my options tomorrow. Somewhere between awake and asleep I decide it might be best for everyone if I just go back to being twenty-eight again.

The morning comes quickly, and after realizing yesterday was not just a dream, I sit up in Gavin's bed and continue writing the piece I started on the stoop last night. I hear cabinets closing and dishes quietly clinking, so I go to the kitchen in search of food and/or coffee.

Gavin is standing in the corner of the very small wall-papered galley kitchen eating a bowl of cereal, wearing only his boxers. His brown hair is sticking up in several different directions and he has a tiny dribble of milk down the stubble on his chin. I enter the kitchen and smile at him but try not to look in his direction as I continue towards a dust-covered coffee maker that is buried under dirty cups and some random junk mail.

He remarks sleepily, wiping the milk off his chin, "Sorry I forgot we had a guest. I usually don't have to put on pants until at least noon."

I flush again and avert my eyes from his bare chest to the floor beneath us.

He turns to set his dirty cereal bowl in the sink, and glancing up at him, I notice a tattoo on his side, under his left armpit. It is a series of symbols that appear to be some other language or something, scrawled in black against his oblique muscle.

"What is that?" I touch him lightly, pointing out the tattoo and he jumps, his bowl making a loud clink on the other dirty dishes in the sink.

"Geezus! What? It's a tattoo."

"What is it of?"

"It's a philosophy. For life."

"How profound of you," I say with a mocking tone and a grin.

He pauses, staring at me with a look I can't figure out, and for a moment I'm worried I offended him.

"I'll show you profound," he smiles, picking me up and throwing me over his shoulder in one quick motion before I have time to react.

Hanging upside down, he holds me around the waist with one arm. I smack him on the back and yell for him to let me go, just like I used to so many years ago. He laughs and drops me onto the couch where he slept. His pillow and blanket are still warm. He turns to head back to the kitchen, and I can't help but laugh and, without thinking, I run up behind him and jump on his back, wrapping my arms and legs around him. He barely moves, since I am so much smaller than him, but he grabs my arms, trying to pry them off of his chest, and in doing so, I start to fall backwards off his back. I fall to the ground behind him, as we both laugh. Then he begins to throw the blanket, pillow, couch cushions, and anything else he can find on top of me, burying me in a mountain of soft, bulky items. I laugh so hard that I'm out of breath, and I yell for him to get me out from under the pile, even though I'm perfectly capable of pushing the weight off of myself.

He doesn't respond, and so I yell again,"Gavin! I need coffee and food! I'm gonna die under here!"

I am still laughing as I feel a very large, rough hand grip my forearm and pull me up out of the pile. I stumble over a cushion awkwardly and lose my balance, but he catches me before I fall back to the ground. I am suddenly pressed up against Gavin for a brief moment, as he steadies me back on my feet. Our faces are only inches apart for a split second, but my hands instinctively land on his chest and push myself back enough that he's forced to loosen his grip. I regret my instinct immediately when I am no longer touching him, my stomach again aching deep inside. I have tears in my eyes and clutch my stomach which I assume must be sore from all the laughter.

"What are you weirdos doing?" Mike asks, limping out from his bedroom and rubbing his eyes.

Gavin quickly steps away from me and begins picking up the blankets and pillows off the ground, "I tried to suffocate your sister after she dissed my tattoo."

"Really?" he pauses and looks at me, "Good call Kendall, that tattoo is super gay."

I laugh again, and Gavin chucks a pillow at Mike, who ducks to miss it.

"What? Don't be all butt-hurt! I told you not to get it."

Gavin runs at my brother and gently and easily puts him in a headlock.

"Dude, I'm injured. Don't take out your closet homosexuality on me. I love you no matter what your preferences are."

I laugh so hard again that I fall to the ground clutching my stomach, "Stop! I can't breathe!"

They both laugh and Gavin releases Mike, who then grabs his crutches from the living room and hops over to the kitchen.

"Well, Ken, since you're here to take care of me, I like my coffee with two sugars and cream."

"Shut up Mike," I snap playfully.

After realizing that the only coffee in their apartment is a can of Folgers that looks like it's been left in the cabinet by a previous tenant, I walk up to a local coffee shop and buy three large cups of Sumatra. The walk back is only about five blocks, but I take my time. The air is cool, and the smell is of fresh soil and newly fallen leaves. Other than the occasional roar of a truck engine, I hear only the sound of my feet against the concrete and a lone bird calling out to the sun. Light bounces off of the distant mountains and the clouds feel like they are floating over me protectively. I am not too cold or too warm, and for once, I'm not thinking about the past few days, or years, or the future. I feel a strange stillness that is completely foreign to me, and all I can think about is how I don't want it to end.

When I return to the boys' apartment, Mike is in the shower and Gavin is standing with his back to me in the hallway, bent over and attempting to pull on giant wool socks. Holding one arm against the wall to prop himself up, he's dressed in snow pants and a hideous old T-shirt with cut-off sleeves. For a second I stare at his arms, remarking to myself how different he looks, and I have to force myself to look away. I'm not sure if he heard me come in but I put the coffees down on the counter and start putting various dishes from the counter into the dishwasher. I know Gavin is still in the hallway across the apartment but I can somehow feel him watching me. I continue cleaning, moving over to the sink to rinse and load more dishes. I brush my hair out of my eyes and looking up we meet eyes again as he walks towards me. I must need some food, because my stomach makes a flip as he gets closer.

He stops several arm lengths back from me, like he is almost afraid to come any closer. He motions to the chair next to him which is draped with snow gear, "Get dressed, we're going to the mountain."

"What? Mike can't go to the mountain—his knee—"

"Mike has PT all day, so I've been designated as your babysitter. And hurry up—it's more crowded the closer it gets to noon."

"Uh—thanks, but, I don't think so. I'll just wait here for Mike. How long is PT?" I've never been snowboarding in my life, and there's a reason for that. It's cold and dangerous and it's not exactly an important life skill I need to acquire to further my ambitions.

"I'm not asking. Get dressed and let's go."

I don't know if it's that I don't want to stay in this dirty apartment alone, or if I just don't feel like arguing, but either way I surprise myself and follow him out to the truck without putting up more of a fight.

When we get out of the car at the first lift, I look up at the massive mountain before me and start to panic. I am so bundled up in layers that I begin sweating, and as I start talking myself out of stepping onto the snow, Gavin shoves a hat over my hair, which is knotted up on top of my head. I now officially look like a terrified twelve-year-old boy.

Gavin bends down to help me clip into Mike's board, which is slightly too big of course, and explains that I am standing goofy-footed. He tells me to keep my legs bent and my butt down, arms out like a stink bug.

"The lower your butt is towards the ground, the less it hurts when you land on it. Let's go."

I nod and shuffle towards the lift, one foot strapped into the board. As the people in front of us board the ski lift effortlessly, we then shift into the next spot closer. But as I attempt to put my feet in a straight line, I slip and nearly face-plant in front of the large line of people waiting. Gavin catches me under my arm, and the entire lift is forced to a stop while I gather myself and scramble over to the moving bench. I feel like I might cry out of embarrassment and fear. Gavin acts oblivious to my concerns as he cleans and straps on his goggles. I'm too nervous to speak, so I just stare at the increasingly distant snow-covered ground below us.

Just before we get to the top of the lift, Gavin helps me clip my second foot in and reminds me about my stance. I'm not able to register any of his words, and I fall immediately out of the lift at the last second. Gavin helps me up again. I brush the snow off my knees and out of my jacket collar, and I follow him very slowly over to the top of the run. I fall twice on the way and scoot on my butt over the snow to finally sit next to him at the top. He pulls me back up on my feet so I'm now facing him, and grabs my hands with his, basically supporting most of my body weight. I feel a tiny bit of relief knowing he's there with me, but then I look down the mountain and freak out all over again. I bite my lower lip, and then I start to completely lose my shit, "Gavin, I—I can't!" the words spit out of my mouth in desperation, as I sink back down into a sitting position in the snow. He looks at me for a second with concern, which quickly shifts to intensity when he realizes I'm not physically hurt.

"You're fine. We're going down this mountain together, and it's going to be fun."

"I can't do it!"

"Yes, you can, Kendall. It's the bunny slope—there are five-year-olds doing it. Just lean towards me and let go."

After spending the better part of my twenties holding on to my independence for dear life, I surprise myself by obeying his instructions and accepting my current dependence on him. I lift myself awkwardly back upright and grab his gloved hands. We creep slowly down the bunny slope, and I fall immediately. Then I fall a half a dozen more times. Gavin patiently waits for me to get up each time and doesn't patronize me by spouting encouraging bullshit. He just holds out his hands silently and we move farther down the hill together. Finally, when I'm about halfway down and back up on my board with my feet underneath me, I actually ride solo for about twenty yards or so. I fall again but this time holding my fists in the air in celebration and looking back at Gavin whose face is lit up with elation. I sit there on my sore butt, exhausted, as he rides over. He stands over me, offering me a gloved hand and a genuine smile.

"Hell yea, Kendall!"

He pulls his goggles up to rest on his forehead and we meet eyes and laugh. My laugh is full of fatigue and relief. I am soaked and sore and uncomfortable, but I rode a freaking snowboard down a mountain. Well, at least part of the way.

32

MIKE

My knee aches and throbs after the session. I feel like a rubber band that's been stretched out too far. My physical therapist says I'm progressing, but it will be a long time before I can run again. And I may never be able to play 'high risk' sports that involve a lot of pivoting, like basketball and of course lacrosse.

This is information that I've been told already, by the surgeons and the doctors that I've seen, but it doesn't make it any easier to hear.

Since it's my left knee I'm still able to drive an automatic. So after PT each week I take my car up Flagstaff and turn off the engine and just sit. For the past few weeks, my thoughts have been occupied by my lack of purpose. I had an idea of how my life might look, at least in the next couple of years. Now that plan is shot to shit. And the way I dealt with my problems in the past was to go running or go practice. So now I'm literally S.O.L.

I turn up the radio to drown out my thoughts, and the music helps a little. The local campus radio station plays some weird shit, but this is tolerable. I close my eyes and try to picture something, anything that will calm my anger and frustration.

If I could just go back in time and fucking drop the pass or throw an assist.

You are acting like a fucking pussy, I think to myself.

As I drive back down into town, I now feel less angry but more empty. Without thinking, I pull into the parking lot of the liquor store and cut the engine.

KENDALL

After a few more runs of sliding down the bunny slope on my butt, I'm finally starting to relax and enjoy the fresh mountain air and the use of my legs which have only been exercised on my daily walk to and from campus and a rare workout on the elliptical. After some negotiations, Gavin convinced me that he should go down the double blue without me, while I practice my balance and butt-landing technique. As the sun begins to set, I squint up into its golden glare to try to spot Gavin on the slope above me. But the snowboarders all look similar in their gear, zig-zagging across the long cast shadows, their forms silhouetted against the white snow. The sunlight shifts from golden to burnt orange, and Gavin appears next to me as if from nowhere. He offers me a hand, and I don't hesitate to take it, my legs grateful for a momentary release from the pull of gravity. Gavin is calm and silent as we walk back to his truck, and I feel a sort of contagious, internal quiet that I'm not used to. I peel off the soaked parka, hat, and snowboarding pants that I borrowed from Mike, and I can barely muster the energy to crawl up into the passenger seat of his truck. I think about the last time I was in here, and how quickly his mom fell asleep—how weak she was. I watch Gavin through the back window as he straps the boards down in the bed of the truck and I am forced to look away, thinking about his future loss and how much pain he must have been in. Or rather, how much pain he will be in.

Gavin slides into the driver's seat and smiles at me as he starts up the truck. I smile back, and blush because I notice him looking down at my ridiculous outfit—composed of Mike's boxer shorts and old mesh tank top from his summer lacrosse league.

"So, you stoked yet?" he asks bobbing his head slightly for emphasis, as we pull onto the road that leads back to their apartment.

I just smile and laugh and watch the campus fly by my window, and I can feel Gavin's eyes darting from the road to me and back again as we turn onto the highway that will lead us back to Boulder. Gavin fiddles with the radio dial, stopping on an indie station and drumming his thumbs against the steering wheel. I'm grateful for the music to fill the truck with something other than awkward silence.

After a few minutes of driving, Gavin lowers the music a bit and glances over at me, then back at the road and asks, "so you like living in New York?"

"Uh, yea—of course. It's the most amazing and vibrant city on the planet."

"I've never been," he adds.

"Seriously? You have to go—it's just a stream of endless energy. I can't even explain it."

"I'll take your word for it."

I pause to consider his response. "Does that mean you don't want to go?"

"No, never said that. I just trust your opinion," he says, looking into my eyes with a genuine but unfamiliar look, like he's intrigued by them.

"It's basically the polar opposite of Sunnyvale," I say, turning back towards the window and crossing my arms.

"Ah, c'mon, Sunnyvale wasn't that bad. I remember some excitement. What about the time you rollerbladed into that parked car?"

"Ohmygod shut-up!" I retort.

"I think Mike carried you about a half-mile back home. You were not just crying, you were like screaming and sobbing about how much you hated everything."

"That was so awful."

"Yea, but now it's such a great story."

"Not to me."

"Why?"

"Because it was so embarrassing! I never rollerbladed again—I sucked so bad."

"You've got to get over yourself," he says, shaking his head with a smirk.

I turn my head quickly, to face him, "Excuse me?"

"Oh, c'mon Kendall. You know what I mean."

"No, I don't."

"When you just chill out and let things go, you are actually fun to be around. Sometimes," he laughs, looking over at me and patting me on the knee. I recoil and smack his hand, meeting eyes with him for a split-second before he looks back at the road ahead of us. My mind fixates on the word *sometimes. More conditions.*

"Screw you, Gavin. I'm fun to be around all the time."

He looks at me with complete skepticism. And then back at the road, unimpressed.

And all in one instant, I unbuckle my seatbelt, turn and slide the window to the truck-bed open, and using my arms, pull myself through in one swift motion, falling in a sort-of tucked ball into the bed of his truck. Gavin swerves, knocking me towards the side of the truck, and I fall against a snowboard.

The air is so loud rushing past my ears that I can barely hear him yell, "What the fuck?" to no one in particular, looking back in the rearview mirror, his mouth agape.

I look back at him with an intense stare and stand up, the cold mountain air whipping around my body and nearly taking my breath out of my lungs. I put my arms out to the side and feel the air pick them up and hold them, giving me the sudden feeling that I'm weightless. I stand like this in the truck bed for a few seconds, my arms outstretched, freezing, but also laughing and feeling invincible for the first time in a decade. There's a strong tug at my torso, and Gavin has gotten his fist around a section of the hem of Mike's old jersey that I'm wearing, and before I can fight him, he's yanked me back through the window and is yelling something inaudible at me, while he pulls the truck over at the next exit.

I'm still laughing, my face somewhat numb and windburned, as he brakes suddenly in a parking lot off to the side of the rest-stop, "Why are we stopping?"

Gavin looks at me, his face twisted with what I suspect might be anger, but I can't pinpoint it because I literally have never seen Gavin angry before.

"Don't ever do that again!" he says, rubbing his face vigorously with his two hands. Pausing with them resting on either side of his jaw, he stares down at the steering wheel and then looks sideways at me.

"What, that wasn't fun for you?" I pant, still out of breath from the bitter cold. I rub my upper arms to smooth away the goosebumps and laugh again, tossing my head back at the ridiculousness of this afternoon.

We lock eyes and his gaze softens a bit. His stupid Gavin-grin takes over his face, and he laughs too, "Well, I can't say I expected that."

"Good," I say, smiling at him. He pauses like he wants to say something, his face moving just slightly towards mine and then turning back towards the steering wheel again.

"Try to stay inside the truck on the rest of the way home, okay? I don't want to have to explain your disappearance to your family."

"Like they would even notice," I say, my smile fading back into the reality of my life. I turn to face back towards my passenger-side window, catching my reflection in the glass.

"What are you talking about?"

"I'm not exactly the model daughter that they hoped for" I frown at myself, "but I guess Mike's joining me in my mediocrity now that he's not a star lacrosse player." I look down at my feet, the beginnings of blisters forming on each and every one of my pink toes.

We ride in silence for a few miles, and on a few occasions I glance in Gavin's direction. His mouth is a straight line and his eyes are glued to the road.

"What's your problem?" I finally ask, annoyed by the fact that I care.

"It's just kind of fucked-up. That you think like that."

I look at him, now with my mouth hanging open, shocked by his words.

"Nobody's perfect, Kendall. And Mike's not just a screw-up like you think he is. He's got issues right now, but he'll get through them."

The deja vu I feel at this very moment feels like a swift kick to my gut. Last time Gavin said that, he stormed off and walked out of my life. And I let him.

The words just spill out of me now, "I'm not trying to be perfect. But I am trying to be better. And if I don't always get better than what am I even doing? What's the point?" I exhale, sinking back into the seat.

"If you don't get the point, I can't explain it to you."

"Why not?"

"There's not enough time," he says, half-smiling at me as we pull into the familiar parking lot of their apartment building.

We unload some of the gear and as soon as we enter the apartment we're greeted by loud, heavy-metal music blaring through the small space. The coffee table is littered with beer cans and chips. Gavin glances at me with what I interpret as a subtle worried look and then goes quickly into his room. I stand in the middle of the living room waiting for his return, and I go over to the stereo and turn the music down, just as Mike barrels into the living room from the bathroom.

"Don't-fucking-touch-my-stereo," he says all in one slurred word, as he stumbles over to the dial and turns the music off. The silence is calming for about a millisecond. Mike makes his way to the kitchen, nearly falling into the fridge, and cracks open a beer. He limps back over to me, while chugging the beer and spilling some onto his shirt. His eyes meet mine, and he has that glazed look like he's not really here—like his mind is conscious, but alcohol has overcome his memory and most of his personality.

"Why'd you turn off the music?" he looks at me, his eyes unable to focus directly on mine. And I know he's not asking as his normal sarcastic self.

I open my mouth to remind him what really happened, but Gavin interrupts me, "Mikey! How's it going brada-man?"

Mike half-smiles at his friend, now with his eyes closed, and stumbles backwards during another swig of his beer.

"Just fucking great, Gavin you fucking chode you..." he trails off, his words a combination of inaudible slurs and gibberish.

I realize that my hands are starting to sweat and I try to wipe them on the shitty old bag that's strapped across my body. I don't handle unpredictable well. As usual, this must be written all over my face because Gavin keeps looking over at me and then continues trying his best to act normal and diffuse the situation.

"Dude, can I have some of that beer? I'm super thirsty," Gavin holds his hand out towards the can, and Mike playfully swats him away.

"Get your own. There's like five kinds in the fridge—shitty, extra light and shitty, and dog piss—" he counts on his fingers slowly, laughs and almost falls over. He catches me watching him and he steadies himself and slams his beer down on the coffee table, spilling a bunch on himself and the carpet, "What the fuck are you looking at?"

I look down at the floor and try to think of something to say, but I'm honestly too scared. I've never been around someone this drunk and angry.

"Mikey, let's go out," Gavin says lightheartedly.

"She's fucking 'too cool for school', Gav, look at her. She's too good for everything," he says with increasing aggression in his voice, stepping towards me.

"Mike, where's the bowl? Let's smoke one."

"I fucking know, Kendall," he points at his temple, "I'm not a retard like you think I am."

He stands over me so closely that I can smell the sharp scent of liquor on his breath. I am so confused and scared that I instinctively step back and try to get around him. He stands in my way, leaning on the wall for support now.

Gavin comes over and slides his shoulder between us, placing one hand on Mike's chest to make sure he stays where he is. Mike ignores him and keeps staring at me. I've never seen my brother like this. It's almost like he's possessed.

"She wrote all about it—how much of a fuck-up I am. How she wants to 'help me' get a real job and make something of myself. I don't need her fucking help," he says to Gavin, while still staring me down.

My lower lip begins to quiver and I have to bite it to make it stop.

"Dude stop, just relax and let's go to the bar."

"Fuck you, man!" Mike yells as he hobbles into Gavin's room. Gavin looks over at me, confused. I can feel tears running down my cheeks, so I rub them away and look in the opposite direction.

I am hit in the stomach by my journal, which then falls to the floor. It was a strong throw, but my shock far exceeds my pain, so all I can do is stand here, holding my stomach and crying.

"She just came here to prove she's still better than me. Guess what? Nobody gives a fuck!" Mike shouts at me.

I can't hold myself together any longer, and so I pick up my journal and run out of the apartment, slamming the door behind me without looking back and sprinting through the parking lot like a maniac. I am audibly sobbing at this point, and I run down their street, ignoring the burning sensation in my tired legs. I should be cold in only shorts and a tank top, but I can only think about my brother's hurtful words and how I will probably never see him again. I slow to a walk, my legs exhausted, and the flood of tears clouding my vision forces me to stop and sit on a curb outside a small restaurant in town. I sit on the concrete ledge, alone and crying, until it feels like there's no tears left.

College students walk by me, some of them looking at me funny and some with concern. I am suddenly very homesick for Manhattan, where no one would even notice me sitting here. And where I never had anyone I cared about this much make me feel this small.

After some time on the curb, my breathing slows and my eyes dry. I remind myself how old I am and tell myself to get my shit together and act like the responsible twenty-eight-year-old that I am. There is always a solution, I tell myself in the hopes that I'll believe it.

I tie my hair up in a knot on top of my head, rub my face with the bottom of my shirt, and start looking through my bag. I have thirty dollars and my parents' emergency credit card. I have no clothes or even a toothbrush, but at least I can use the card to get the hell out of this place. After what feels like an eternity, I find the only cab in Boulder and flag it down.

"Airport, please."

I pay for the cab with the cash and make my way through the Boulder airport. I don't even look at the cost for a ticket back to JFK. I decide I'll just take another cab to that freaking building, get in the elevator and never look back. I can't believe how stupid I've been and how much time I've wasted.

If I can ever get back, will time pick up where I left off? Or will I wake up a week after I left and have missed my opportunity to meet Susan Wilder?

Whatever happens, at least I will have my apartment and my career and my sanity back.

—

As I'm leaning against a pole waiting for my plane, hugging myself to keep warm and watching the puddle-jumpers take off over the mountains, a kind-faced elderly woman stops in front of me to offer me a jacket. I force a fake smile but shake my head. She looks like she wants to continue talking to me, but I put in a pair of headphones and look past her to the runway. She takes the hint and shuffles away, and I immediately feel regret and sadness about my habitual coldness. I wasn't always this way—it's been a slowly learned behavior after years of self-preservation. Since I couldn't control other people, I started choosing to avoid them rather than live in constant battle with myself.

After a few minutes, my stomach pangs with hunger, and so I make my way over to a set of vending machines for anything resembling food. I walk by a coffee kiosk, several crappy fast food places, and to the other end of the terminal, closer to the security gate.

As I'm perusing the pseudo-food options before me, I hear someone shout my name. I wheel around, shocked, and from behind a middle-aged couple, Gavin appears. He approaches me slowly, leaving the security area with his shoes and wallet in his hand. His face is more serious than I have ever seen it. I am stunned and frozen.

He drops his shoes on the ground in front of me, looking down at his feet and slipping them on, and shoves his wallet in his back pocket. He still doesn't smile, which I realize makes his face look older and more mature, but also a little foreign.

As his eyes meet mine, I am the first to speak, "What are you doing here?"

He looks down at me, and his eyes are full of something that I don't recognize, "Why are you leaving?"

I don't have an answer, and I'm distracted by trying to interpret his face. I look at him and then down at myself, "Mike hates me. It's too late."

"What's too late?"

"I—I don't know. You wouldn't believe me if I told you."

He steps closer to me and puts his hand on my shoulder awkwardly, and then changes his mind and shoves it into his jeans pocket.

"Mike's just wasted. You can't take it personally. He's going through some rough shit right now. Just come back with me. We'll sort it out."

I don't say anything, but I shake my head in disbelief and look away.

"And I would believe you."

I look down at my plane ticket and back at him, "I've—I've been so naive and so insane and I need to get back to my real—my actual—" I don't want him to see me start to cry again so I turn around and face the window behind us, my voice cracking, "I just can't take it anymore."

"Kendall, I—"

"What do you want?" I ask him, sounding like a small child who is frustrated with my inability to articulate anything out loud.

My tears have halted and now I just feel ashamed of everything. Of thinking I could make amends with Mike—thinking that he'd want to see me after all this time.

Then I feel a large hand engulf the bend in my arm, and it pulls me backwards gently but firmly. I spin around, off-balance and Gavin leans down and presses his lips roughly to mine. He pulls me against him, giving me no time to hesitate. Then I realize I am kissing him back, and suddenly there is nothing else. No thoughts of self-doubt or of anxiety. It is only Gavin, and a strong yearning deep in my gut that forces me to pull him in closer and closer until I feel like there is no space between us. He puts his hand in my hair and holds the back of my head firmly, kissing me deeper.

He slowly lets go of my head and pulls his mouth off of mine, and I am so dizzy that I feel weightless. He looks at me and smiles, and kisses me lightly again. I find myself kissing him back and this time I am the one that will not let him pull away. He holds most of my weight against him with his right arm around my waist and then presses his left hand up against the window behind me for support. He releases his grip a little and pulling back a few inches, looks me in the eyes.

"I want—I've been trying—" he pauses, "I just want to be near you all the time. It's weird."

I look at his eyes and at first I think I can tell he is being genuine. My stomach flutters again. A shrill phone ring interrupts us, and Gavin breaks eye contact with me, looking down at his pocket. The ringing repeats itself, and he backs up, reaching down to answer the call. Then my conscious mind kicks back into gear—he is just a confused twenty-one-year-old boy who is attracted to me and hasn't really thought past his hormones. I am twenty-eight and I've been through this already. It will get ugly when he finds out I'm not exactly what he wants me to be.

He pushes a button, silencing the ring. Over the loud-speaker, they announce that some random flight is boarding. I don't even know what is said, but I take the opportunity and lie, "That's my flight. I need to go."

I don't look at Gavin's face, I just pull back and look at my folded arms beneath me.

Then he asks me the most complicated simple question, "What do you want, Kendall? I mean, why did you really come here?"

I don't have an answer that makes any kind of logical sense, so I don't speak. There is some truth to his words, that I'm the one who decided to show up on their doorstep for some reason that is now unclear to me. *To use my brother to help me travel back to my future life?*

I look at him with more regret and even more sadness, and then I walk away from him without looking back. I enter the women's restroom, then a stall, and close the door behind me, locking it. I turn and stare at the back of the blank metal door. I am too exhausted to cry, so I just stare at the dents and scratches from years of use. I run my hands over the door, ignoring the fact that it is probably covered in germs, and am reminded of the elevator. That fucking elevator. I would give anything to have taken the goddamn stairs.

His hand on my head.

I tried. I tried to make things right with Mike— I tried to appease my mother and be a good sister and daughter.

His smell of outside and Old Spice.

I will never be good enough. I'm too damn selfish.

His stubble on my lips.

The troll was right. My life is empty.

And the tears begin again.

After convincing and unconvincing myself to leave the bathroom close to a dozen times, and composing myself a bit, I looked for Gavin at each terminal, restaurant, bookstore, and kiosk. He was gone. So I bought a *Boulder, Colorado* sweatshirt with a picture of a cartoon bear, and slept in a horribly uncomfortable chair at the airport until my five AM flight left.

And now after the thirty-five-minute cab ride to go only two miles through the city, I walk into the lobby of the building where it all began. It's bustling with people arriving for another day of work. No one really notices me, in my random combination of men's ill-fitting gym clothes, and I'm relieved. I decide to avoid the crowds and wait in the lobby until the elevator is empty, but as I wait idly, my mind starts up again. Instead of having a panic attack right here in the lobby of this office building, I decide to get out my journal and write a story. It is a simple story, about an invisible woman who goes through life thinking she is seen. She then finally discovers her own invisibility, and that any impact she had on people around her was actually circumstantial, and she turns to a life of travel and freedom because of her gift. Then her life is unexpectedly cut short when she is run over by a bus that never even knew she was there.

When I look up from my scribbling, I realize that the lobby is quiet and there is only the distant sound of the air conditioning running. I walk slowly over to the elevator bank and push the *UP* arrow. I have this empty, numb feeling that is all encompassing. I will myself to just keep moving forward and enter the elevator alone. The doors close and my despair weighs so heavily, that I don't even feel like lifting my arm to push the top button. It doesn't matter though, because the floor beneath me starts moving up anyway. My eyes start to well up again, and I realize how naive I've been. I've never been in control of this journey. All this time I thought these detours were accidental, but it's clear now that I never had a choice. And here I am, alone again, with no one to explain it to and no one who would ever even believe me. There is a ding and the doors open on the third floor.

33
YEAR 3

MIKE

Kendall won't get out of bed. I ran in her room and tried to scare her and tickle her and make her giggle and she didn't want to play. I told Mommy and now Mommy and Daddy seem scared. I am playing with my firetruck and my tractor and it is great. I am the fireman and the farmer needs me to save his horse from the bad guys. Daddy tells me to come downstairs for lunch, and I ask him where Kendall is, and he says she's still sleeping. Then Mommy and Daddy take me over to Gavin's house to play, and it's the best day ever. Mommy and Daddy and Kendall go somewhere else in the car. While they're gone Gavin's mom gives us freezer pops and we play with Gavin's GI Joes. I don't want to stop playing, but Daddy comes back in to get me after a while and tells me it's time to go home. I get in the car, and Kendall is still sleeping. Mommy and Daddy talk about a doctor and nurse and what they said about Kendall. I don't know what they mean so I ask them, and they tell me Kendall saw Dr. Miller today.

"Did she get a shot?" I say, very scared for her.

"No, honey. She is just very sleepy and Dr. Miller is trying to figure out why."

"Maybe she drank too much soda and then she couldn't sleep last night and now she's too tired to stay awake."

"Maybe so, Mikey."

Mommy pulls Kendall out of her car seat and holds her while we all walk up the driveway. It's dark, and I don't like the dark, so I hold Mommy's leg while Daddy unlocks the front door.

I follow them into Kendall's room and watch her lay her into bed and tuck her in, and she kisses her forehead and looks sad. Maybe it will help Kendall if I kiss her forehead too, so I lay next to her in her bed and kiss her hair and give her a big hug. I love my little sister, and I hope she wakes up soon. But if not, maybe tomorrow Gavin and I can play Cops 'n Robbers.

KENDALL

I wake up in my twin bed from childhood with a quilt pulled up to my chin, surrounded by stuffed animals. Without really thinking, I jump out of bed and run across my room, and it takes so many steps to get to the door, which looks gigantic. I can barely turn the doorknob when I'm on my tiptoes. It's strange to have twenty-eight years of insight and experience in such an awkward and inexperienced physical state. Every step I take feels like I could fall down at any moment. I peek out of the cracked bedroom door and hear my parents' voices hushed across the hall, making out only the words "—hasn't eaten anything all day—"

The voices then move towards me, so I scurry quickly back to my bed and bury myself under the covers.

Praying they leave me alone, I try my best to close my eyes and fall back asleep. I am just so exhausted and hopeless—I want to sleep forever and never wake up.

I discover a few hours later that a three-year-old does not have the luxury of being depressed. Since I've spent the better part of the last twenty-four hours in bed, it is assumed that I am extremely sick, so I'm taken to the emergency room and I have to prove that I am not deathly ill by faking normalcy. I pretend to play a little with my stuffed animal and force a laugh at Mike when he makes faces at me, even though laughing seems impossible right now. The nurse gives me a popsicle, but I really don't feel like eating. However, after there's talk of a feeding tube, I shovel it down as fast as I can. My mom's face looks relieved, and Mike tries to steal a bite while we all sit waiting for the doctors to let us leave.

—

On the way home, we drive through San Jose, and it's very different than in the years I've been there lately. The eBay campus is just an old dilapidated office building and a parking lot, and there is no sign of the Silicon Valley social media companies that will eventually dominate the town. Time is such a strange phenomenon.

It can change so much context, but context that I now realize is mostly driven by the whims of humans. Buildings, shops, gas stations, television, clothes, cars—these are the things that change so dramatically between decades but the natural landscape beyond them is relatively stagnant. At least for much longer than my twenty-eight years on this earth.

This idea, that our impact on time is so minimal compared to the universe, gives me a shred of hope. Hope because then the pressure is off—maybe this journey could be just a crazy cosmic accident. I found a worm hole between two buildings with twenty-eight floors. And if I just keep trying to find my way back to it, I'll eventually make it back to the present.

We pass my dad's work building and turn into the detached parking garage behind it, which I've become very familiar with over this past week. I ask my mom why we're going to his office, and she says that he wants to see me, which means I must've really worried him. They probably thought it was cancer or something, and part of me wishes it was.

No, I take that back, I say to myself, thinking of Gavin and pushing him back out of my head all in the same instant.

Kendall, look at me sweetie. It's okay, I'm here, her soft voice says to me in between sobs.

She won't stop crying, Mom.

It's okay. She'll be okay, Ms. Bennett says, stroking my hair, *Gavin, honey, go get an ice pack. Mike, call your mom and tell her what happened.*

My sobs slow to tears and an occasional sniffle, as I hold my leg at the shin, afraid to let go.

Can you move it, sweetheart?

I...don't...think...so, I croak, out of breath still from my hysterics.

Gavin returns with a giant ice pack and his mom places it gently over my swollen ankle. She tells the boys a few more instructions as I calm down further, and Mike says that my mom is on her way.

Mike and Gavin leave us alone in the kitchen, and I've finally stopped crying long enough to drink a few sips of the water that Gavin's mom offered me.

You know, when I was about your age I knocked out my two front teeth trying to ride my bike over a curb. Man, it hurt so bad. I was bleeding everywhere, and I had to walk around for a few weeks with no front teeth! she says, demonstrating by covering her front teeth with her index finger. I smile weakly in response. *But you know, that next week was Halloween, and because of my missing teeth, I won the costume contest. So without that crazy accident I never would have had so much fun. And now when I look back, I just laugh and laugh. It's one of my favorite stories to tell.*

What did you dress up as?

Rocky. I had a big fake black-eye and blood everywhere. I looked so great.

Who's Rocky?

He's a boxer—oh, it's not important, she gently wipes my face with a cool, damp cloth.

Why do you like telling the story so much?

Hmm—I don't know, she looks me in the eye and smiles, *I guess because when I don't take myself so seriously, there's a lot of laughter to be had out of all the craziness in this world.*

I was nine-years-old when Ms. Bennett helped clean me up after my rollerblading accident, and I will never forget how calm, kind and comforting she was. But what I failed to remember until now was her lightness. And ironically, it's probably the trait I need most in my own life.

I hold my mom's hand as we walk through the massive and loud parking garage. I have to practically run to keep up with her, and as I look up and watch her walking, I realize that I look a lot more like her at this age than I ever thought. It's hard to remember that my parents were once young, full of dreams and ambition and energy. My mom can't be more than thirty, only slightly older than my real age, or what it should be, and she already has two kids, balances maintaining a house and raising us, and takes classes part time at night for her teaching certificate. And she selflessly puts aside her own needs for ours every day. When my young mother notices that I am staring up at her, she looks down at me and smiles.

We all hold hands in a line as we cross the street. Mike sings a song that I don't recognize and darts towards the street, as my mom scolds him and grabs him forcefully under the arm. We walk into the lobby and up to the elevators, and my mom is distracted by Mike carrying on and whining. As the elevator doors open, I say a little prayer to myself that this might be the time I finally get to the right floor.

34
YEAR 11

KENDALL

I walk out of the elevator slowly, realizing my hand that was holding my mother's is now holding a small shopping bag. In front of me is the food court of the shopping mall near my childhood home in Sunnyvale. The plastic bag rustles, and I look down at my white knuckles. My slender hands are squeezing the life out of it. My nails are covered in chipped glitter nail polish, I'm wearing my hideous old Sambas, and I have on my favorite neon pink top with no evidence whatsoever of womanly curves underneath. I'm guessing by this location and the fact that I'm prepubescent that I'm here with my mother, and so I wander through the middle of the shopping mall looking for some sign of her.

Right on cue, a sea of angsty teenagers parts and my mom waves at me from a table in the middle of the food court. She excitedly picks up her shopping bags and heads my direction.

"So, what did you get?" my mom asks, attempting to hide her anxiety about letting me shop alone for an unknown duration of time. I can tell she is fighting some kind of internal urge to adjust things on my person, because she lifts and lowers her right hand several times unnaturally.

I look down at the crumpled plastic bag and shrug, "Gray's Sports Almanac."

She looks at me blankly, her smile fading. Knowing that she would never understand my joke, and that it might prompt a series of inquiries, I reach in the bag and pull out a compact flashlight, small enough to fit inside a pocket. She smiles with relief and pats my shoulder, while I try to stifle my frustration that I am back in the wrong time again.

—

We drive through Sunnyvale on this typical California day. The blue sky is streaked with white cotton, the sun relentless, and the attractive, smiling families move quickly past the car window with their dogs and their bikes and their kids, practically glowing with tans and satisfaction. You would think their happiness would be contagious, but I only remember how it worsened my teenage inferiority complex. Now, I still feel a small twinge of envy but not because they are beautiful and perfect, but because they don't seem to care. They aren't taking selfies to show their Instagram followers, or looking over at the cars passing by to make sure the passengers are paying attention to their good time. They are just—together.

As we pass by the entrance to our neighborhood, I search my mind for where we might be heading, but I'm at a loss. My strongest memories of this age consist of riding home with my mom after school, trying to avoid divulging the details of my personal life, and ignoring her tips for self-esteem improvement. When we would get home, she'd quiz me on my homework or about my Bible verses from Sunday's youth group meeting. Mike would then return from soccer or lacrosse practice via Gavin's mom, who used to pick them up on the way home from work. He always smelled like sweat and grass and faintly of cigarettes when he got home. My mom had been pretty good friends with Gavin's mom, but she often told us she didn't approve of some of her choices. How very Christian of her.

We pull up to my old middle school that's a combination of faded red brick and small, opaque windows. There are four sets of blue double doors out front, repainted over decades and decades of use. I get out of the car and approach them, and I don't think it's an optical illusion that they actually look much smaller to me than ever before. I reach out to open one but my mom shouts through the open car window to me.

"They're around back, near the gym, Kendall!" she shakes her head, indicating I should have known this.

I walk around to the right of the building, but Mike's nowhere to be found. I loop around the back, and I find him and Gavin throwing lacrosse balls against the outside wall of the cafeteria, inches from the windows. My heart is in my throat, and not because I'm worried about the glass.

"What are you doing here, spaz?" Mike asks. He pretends to throw a ball at my head and I flinch.

I barely manage to squeak out four words, "Mom's parked around front."

I look at Gavin. He's lanky and awkward—a few pimples lining his chin where in a few years some stubble will be. His face is long and thin, but his bright eyes are the same.

"Race ya to the car, dork!" Gavin yells at Mike, checking his stick to knock out the ball, and they both take off running around the building. I follow, but slowly walking behind them, still thinking about what happened between the three of us less than forty-eight hours ago.

We pile into the car and head to Carl's Jr for burgers, and as we wait in the drive-thru, we are all silent like families who spend a lot of time together often are. Mike rides in the front seat, and Gavin and I are in the back. I try to act like what I think of as a normal eleven-year-old, but I don't remember anything about this age other than how awful everything felt—like you were constantly standing naked in public, a crowd of people taunting you. Thankfully, having developed my frontal cortex over almost two decades, I don't feel quite as exposed. But my vulnerability to what this thirteen-year-old boy potentially thinks about me is equally as alarming.

I look down at my knobby knees and the peach fuzz on my shins. I look over at Gavin's legs which barely have any sign of muscle or hair yet. My mind is full of a strange combination of nervous energy and relief. For one thing, the physical part of being an eleven-year-old is definitely not as terrible as it was the first time—since now I know with certainty that there is an end to the terribleness of puberty. I can mentally find solace in the fact that I don't peak early and have boobs in eighth grade like a lot of the popular girls in middle school who end up either pregnant or with herpes. Or both.

We drop off Gavin, and as he's getting out of the car he thanks my mom for the ride and runs inside his house without even looking in my direction. As we ride through our neighborhood towards the house, I find myself sliding towards his end of the bench seat to feel the warmth from where he was sitting. Mike plays with the radio in the front seat, and his knees bounce to the rhythm of the music. The sun dances across his and my mom's faces as it weaves its way through the trees that line our neighborhood, making a spotty, strobe-like pattern in the car's interior. A thought pops into my brain, almost like someone or something places it there, as we approach our driveway—I miss this.

My mom shuts off the engine, forcing my mind back to the interior of the car, and the two front doors swing open almost in sync. My mom and brother silently unload their stuff and file through the garage into the house leaving me in the back of the car without so much as a second look.

Their leaving me here doesn't make me feel abandoned or even upset, but rather makes me feel as if I'm a complete stranger to myself. I used to long to be away from these people, and bitter at even the prospect of a forced conversation with them. But now I can't seem to extricate myself from my past, and even at these rare moments when I have an empty car and no one holding me back, I still want to follow them inside. And I begin to think that without them I'm missing an important piece of some universal puzzle.

My eyes are tired and glassy from all this speculation. I crawl out of the back seat of the car and slowly up the garage stairs into my parents' kitchen. I can hear the shower running in Mike's and my shared bathroom, and I wait around in my room. I stare at the stick-on stars on my ceiling, longing to explain myself to my older brother. But when I try to think of what I might say to a thirteen-year-old boy, my mind is a blank. After several minutes of useless star gazing, I decide it's probably hopeless and I should just get some rest. Of course my brain won't allow anything close to that. My mind runs around the room and back again.

Since two days ago was chronologically later than today, does Mike still hate me? Or will he?

I seem to be tumbling through time with no real control over anything that happens, and after I re-experience these repressed memories, mostly involving my older brother, I then always end up at an elevator. A portal or black hole or whatever astrophysicists would like to call it. But the elevator always opened to different buildings, and in different years of my life—which does not seem physically possible. And not only that, when I exit the elevator sometimes I never even originate from a different one. There has to be some other reason behind this phenomenon, or maybe I can discover a pattern to what I hope is not my own madness. I rifle through my desk for anything to write on or in, and I struggle but eventually come across an old diary that only had a few pages filled in. I start writing what I know to be true about the past few days:

> *-I am not always going forward or going backward in time*
> *-I always end up back in the elevator*
> *-My choice of floor does not determine where I'm going*
> *-I somehow end up finding Mike*
> *-Gavin remembers my prediction of the blackout both in the past and years after*
> *-Changing minor things in previous years does not create an alternate universe in later years*

...What about major things?

This whole journey, I've had a healthy fear of making anything but small changes to my past decisions. The first major change was when I stood up to the Asshole, but he was never a part of my life after that night, at least physically. But what about later when I decided to break up with Chris and detour to Boulder? That break-up was inevitable anyway. So did I really change anything major that would not have happened anyway?

Oh no, I think, *the kiss.*

Suddenly I hear a crash that sounds like it came from Mike's room.

35

MIKE

"Dammit," I whisper to myself as I start to clean up the pieces of the ceramic cup I made in elementary school art class. I pick up the whole desk that I managed to knock over onto the floor and wait for my mom to barrel into my room wondering what happened. Even moving the entire desk out, I still can't find what I'm looking for.

I swear I hid them there.

I try to act normal after the loud crash, and so I sit on my desk chair lacing a new lacrosse stick head. I don't hear anyone moving around upstairs so I go back to looking in my closet, and, from under an old jersey from summer league, I see the packaging peeking out.

I quickly throw them in the bottom of my bag and cover them with clothes. Downstairs I can hear someone moving around, probably my mom. There's no way to get out of this house without her noticing, so I go with the sly, casual conversation option for my exit.

"Hey, Mom," I begin as I stroll over to the fridge to grab a string cheese, "Gavin invited me to sleep over. Can I go?"

"Tomorrow's a school day, Michael."

"Yeah, but Gavin's mom said she'd take us. And I promise I won't stay up late. *Please.*"

"If you promise me no rated-R movies, and you are in bed by ten."

I roll my eyes internally and agree to her terms. Her creativity is lacking.

I grab my lacrosse stick as I usually would and run my bike out to the street, taking off without looking back.

Tonight's gonna be epic.

KENDALL

I've been trailing Mike on my pink Barbie bike—staying about a half of a block behind him so that I'm certain he doesn't notice me. I don't exactly have a clear rationale for following him, but I'm curious about where he's going in such a hurry. And since I've now determined that all of this time travel always leads back to my brother, I figure it can't hurt to stick around him and see if I can find a pattern to this chaos.

Mike turns into Gavin's cul-de-sac and I wait behind a large tree. He drops his bike and runs up to the side door, I can see Gavin's mom let him in. If I were to describe Gavin's childhood home in one word it would be: brown. Now, I realize, a similar brown to the color of his eyes. The siding is a slightly lighter mocha color than the brown shutters and chocolate door. The yard is brown, the mulch lining the front flowerbeds is brown. The only color comes from a tiny patch of overgrown pansies that line the front stoop, their happy yellow poking through the brown dirt. Inside I remember a bit more variation—the walls are a standard beige color, lined with family photos, shadow boxes with dried flowers, and little trinkets on shelves. Like my parent's house, the sunlight always seemed to be filtered through ruffled curtains, blocking the natural light and creating a dimness that felt simultaneously comforting and tired.

I wait and wait, and the boys don't come back out. It's really strange during this type of warm and long evening that they haven't come outside to toss the ball around or skateboard or something. Practically their entire lives were spent outdoors, pushing their physical limits much like boys do and never ever sitting still. Feeling like something must be off, I decide to lean my bike up against the tree and investigate. I dart quickly over to the side door of the house. I slowly turn the door knob and ease it open. The interior is silent, so I enter and tiptoe towards the exit of the dimly lit linoleum kitchen, leading me into the foyer, and then scurry up the brown-carpeted stairs. I turn left at the top and hide quickly in the first room I can find. I crouch behind the door and scan the room. The benefit of being an eleven-year-old is that I can hide almost anywhere and my footsteps are practically inaudible.

After a few minutes of crouching in my hiding spot behind the door, my legs are starting to go numb. I haven't heard even the slightest sound, so I'm fairly confident that no one else is nearby, including the boys. I stand and stretch out a bit, thinking about my next steps. I've got to hurry if I'm going to catch up with Mike. Clearly after my first nineteen years of life, there were too many complications and complexities for our relationship to overcome. But without the burden of late adolescence, maybe there might still be a tiny window for us to—I don't know—like each other a little? And then, hopefully that will somehow help me get back home.

I glance around the room and there is a queen-sized bed with a purple-flowered bed skirt. There are a few bottles of perfume on the dresser, along with photos of a young Gavin fishing and an even younger young Gavin making funny faces at the camera.

It must be strange to be an only child, I think to myself as I feel a pang of guilt about my own deteriorated relationship with Mike. So many years lost between us—which I never even considered to be missing before.

Can you really lose something you never thought mattered in the first place?

Then I think about a few short days ago, when Gavin held his mother's withered body and helped her walk the short distance from the truck to the house. I think about the pain he must've felt a few years later when she finally took her last breath, and I am physically nauseous to think of Gavin grieving his mother. I touch the framed photograph of him so many years ago, and my hand sends the photo crashing to the ground under my feet. Luckily the floor is carpeted, so the glass doesn't break. I scramble down to pick it up and run into the closet to hide in case someone heard the thump. While I'm bent down peeking through the slats of the closet, I shift my weight from my left to right foot and my elbow knocks over several cartons of Marlboro Lights.

36

MIKE

Joey and Mark are riding over to Gavin's soon and we are all gonna sneak out to the clearing when Gavin's mom is distracted by *Seventh Heaven*. Last summer, we visited my Grandpa in Lake Tahoe and I used the last of my allowance to buy them. I've been waiting and waiting for the right time, and tonight is the perfect night.

After the sun dips down past the horizon, I strap my backpack on and ride behind Gavin towards the hill. Joey and Mark follow and keep an eye out. Mark has a really awesome bike that his mom bought him a few years ago. I wish my parents were divorced so I could get cool stuff. We park the bikes against a tree, and I unzip my bag revealing three huge roman candles.

The guys eyes are huge, and Gavin literally hops and claps at the sight of them.

"Awesome, dude," Joey remarks, "where the heck did you get them?"

"I've been hiding them in my room. I bought 'em in Tahoe when my mom wasn't looking."

Mark reaches out to try and grab one, and I yank back my bag, "Don't touch them!"

"Alright, chill out. Are we gonna shoot them off or what? We have to get back before my mom notices we're gone."

I line the fireworks up on the hill, making sure they are facing the same direction and step back to look at the now-darkened sky above them.

"This is gonna be so nuts!" I exclaim, running back over to wear the guys are standing about twenty yards away.

We stand there awkwardly grinning, and finally Mark asks, "Are you gonna light them?"

"Gav, give me the lighter!" I yell at Gavin, already knowing what his response will be.

"What lighter?" he asks, clueless.

"Dude, you forgot the lighter? Seriously? I told you—"

"You guys are so lame," Mark barks, starting back towards his bike, "C'mon Joey let's go watch Cinemax before my mom gets back from her date."

The two of them ride off, and Gavin just looks at me, confused, "You didn't say anything about a lighter, man."

"I know. C'mon—we can light them another night."

We both hang our heads and start grabbing our stuff.

KENDALL

I ran as fast as I could, down the stairs, and out to the garage when I saw the boys hop on their bikes again from Gavin's mom's bedroom window. In the garage, I rummaged through the shelves and grabbed a small shovel and some matches. I found an old paper bag and shoved them inside with the three cartons of cigarettes and took off running.

I couldn't catch them, so now I'm carrying the bag in one arm and my shoes in the other as I wade through the stream in near darkness, praying that they are in their spot. My heart slows a bit as I hear voices in the distance.

I watch the exchange from behind a tall pine tree and as soon as the other boys leave I can see what they were all standing around. I hear Gavin talk about a lighter and Mike looking disappointed as he packs up his bag, tossing the unlit fireworks in angerly.

"Hey!" I yell as I jog up the hill towards Mike and Gavin. Mike looks at me and his face twists with anger as he quickly zips the bag and hides it behind him.

"What are you doing here, Kendall? This is our secret spot, and you're not allowed! Go home!"

I'm out of breath and I stop a few feet from them and drop my stuff dramatically on the grass. I reach in the bag, and rummage through it for a second.

"Hey! Are you deaf? I said, get out of here!"

I look up at Mike and just smile, and then I light a match.

The boys both look down at me dumbfounded, and then at each other.

Gavin speaks first, "How did you—"

He is silenced by Mike stepping towards me and grabbing the matchbox from my hands. Mike looks down at the bag in his other hand and back at me, and a huge smile sneaks out, taking over his face.

Gavin starts to laugh and they both start setting out the roman candles again. They space them evenly apart and far away from the trees.

"Kendall! Get back!" Mike yells at me while laughing and running towards the tree I am squatting next to. Gavin follows quickly behind. All I can hear are three mouths panting and a faint hissing sound, and then the sky is illuminated. Over and over and over, flashes of red and yellow bounce all over the hillside and the trees and Mike and Gavin cheer loudly.

I watch the light fade against their ecstatic faces, and I feel a warm sensation in my chest that feels like it could erupt at any moment.

They light the next one, and then the next, and we all sit by the big tree and wait for the show to fade. Then they go over with their flashlights to assess the charred remains and celebrate by stomping them into the dirt. It is so quiet, all I can hear is their laughter bouncing all around the clearing. I have this overwhelmingly satisfied feeling that I was just part of something special. So I do a tiny little dance, spinning in a circle with my arms outstretched.

I look down at my feet and suddenly remember how young I am and what I came here for. Next to my sneakers is the paper bag full of cigarettes and the shovel. I look over at Gavin who is laughing and stomping around, and I start to dig.

I dig a small hole and bury the cigarettes as quickly as I can, covering the fresh dirt with pine straw and leaves before the boys return with the flashlights. I had intended to burn them, but this will do.

The flashlight shines on my face. "Kendall? You coming or you sleeping out here?" Mike then tilts the light down at our feet and I can see his big wide grin. "C'mon let's go home before Mom freaks out."

He holds his hand out to help me to my feet, and I follow the two boys back through the dark woods.

I ride on Mike's handle bars down the neighborhood streets that are lit only by the moon and stars, and I hold his flashlight out so he can see where he's going.

I jump off when we get to my front yard, and nearly fall on my face. But I'm too elated to be embarrassed.

"We've gotta go back to Gavin's," Mike says, looking me in the eye, "You remember what I told you to tell Mom?"

I nod and run across the neatly manicured lawn into the house, looking momentarily back at Gavin who is peddling away quickly into the darkness. I turn and run into the living room where I knew my parents would be waiting worriedly and do my best to fake-cry. I unload my story onto them, how I got lost on my bike and how some mean kids stole it and I spent hours wandering around until I could find our house. My mom smooths my hair sympathetically and surprisingly buys all of it. When I look into her eyes, which are full of sympathy and concern, I feel—loved.

I know that I'm an awful human being for causing my parents so much worry, then lying to them and also for helping my thirteen-year-old brother potentially start a catastrophic forest fire, but as I lay here in my tiny bedroom and look up at the glow-in-the-dark stars again, I feel a sense of contentment with this evening's events. I made Mike happy, even if only for a moment, and, if things work out the way I hope, I will also keep Gavin's heart from breaking.

37

KENDALL

As wonderful as bonding with my brother was last night, and also how nice it would be not to have to worry about rent and bills and other adult-related crap—there's still no way in hell I'm going through puberty a second time. And now I'm dying to see the results of my experiment with the cigarettes. So when my dad is busy shaving and getting his bag together for work, and my mom is out speed-walking with a neighbor, I sneak out of my bedroom and hide in the back of the Volvo under a blanket. My dad, who is not really a morning person, goes through the robotic motions of his commute, and it's nearly effortless hitching a ride with him as he sips his coffee and switches the radio between NPR and sports talk.

We arrive at the parking garage, and he gets out and locks the car door behind him. After his footsteps are no longer audible on the pavement outside, I use my cereal-box watch to time five minutes and wait silently in my hiding spot as the seconds tick by. Time measured in small increments, going forward. This is what mankind invented to make sense of the chronology of the universe. Of the movement of the Earth around the Sun.

Tick. Tock.

There is no taking the seconds back. Millions of people have tried to freeze time, whether it be to soak up more time with their loved ones or stop it from etching lines across their faces, but it never stops for them. And it still hasn't truly stopped for me.

Since my dad parked in the center row, it's pretty dark, but I peek out of the rear window anyway. There's no one around, so I slowly roll out of my position in the hatchback of the Volvo. I unlock and push open the car door slowly and then hurry out, careful to lock the door again behind me. The garage is a mass of concrete and oil stains, and I say a small prayer to myself that no one questions where my parents are as I walk by the exit booth with the attendant inside. Taking a deep breath, I quickly shuffle down the sidewalk towards the familiar building. I spent most of the night brainstorming a good reason why an eleven-year-old girl would be showing up at the largest office building in San Jose alone and I came up with nothing. So my plan is now 'not having a plan', and just bolting towards the elevators before the security guard sees me. I figure if I get caught I'll just repeat another version of last night's performance.

I stand outside the building and stare up at the monstrosity of metal and glass and think about the irony of all of this. I've been granted the gift of time-travel but I can't stop trying to get back to the present. And I can never seem to get where I want to be. If only I could choose where I was going, I'd pick a specific place and time and at least do something important— stop Al Qaeda from hijacking those planes or warn people about the Tsunami, or save the children at Sandy Hook. But no, instead I have no control over where I end up.

What good is this? What good am I?

A high-pitched female voice off to my left jolts me back from my internal frustration, and I see a group of students being corralled by their field trip chaperone over onto the front steps of the building. It's my one and only chance, and I take it. I grab a spot in the back and blend in seamlessly with the group, making my way over to the elevator banks with them.

"Okay, everyone! Attention! Raise your hand if you need to use the restroom before we go upstairs?" the middle-aged, slightly overweight woman says in a loud voice, her right hand raised to the sky in demonstration. There are at least five small hands that lift hesitantly around me, and as a result, the group divides, giving me an opportunity to break off. I hide behind a large gentleman with a briefcase who is having a heated argument on the phone and keeps spiking his gelled hair higher and higher with his hand. I sneak onto the elevator on his heels, and for once I do look back. All I see are people in a hurry to get places, and no one's stopping to look around.

<DING>

38
YEAR 23

KENDALL

I open my eyes and my face is resting partially on my arm and partially on a cold, hard surface. I lift my head upright, and I'm next to a monstrous window. Light streams in through the tall trees and into my sleepy eyes. I rub my eyes, and stretch my neck out, and as I glance to my right I notice a young guy with a ponytail sitting beside me and bouncing his knee. He sits a few feet from me at a desk, with headphones on, and types quickly on a laptop. Luckily, he doesn't look up and notice that I'm staring at him. Down the window-lined corridor ahead of me are rows and rows of books, and a young woman walks towards us with a backpack on. Scattered throughout the large, window-lined room there are modern desks, most empty, save for the few containing young women and men with laptops.

I look down at my clothes and I'm wearing ripped jeans, a baseball tee and flip flops. I have a sleek, silver laptop open in front of me, on the desk I was apparently just sleeping on, and look at my reflection in the darkened computer screen. I can tell I am no longer a pre-teen, and my hair is still well beyond my shoulders, but I'm unable to tell what age I am because I'm completely out of context. I have no recollection of this place. I used to study in the library for a few months before I took the bar exam, so I tell myself I must be back in New York, perhaps during my first year of blogging? But these clothes I'm wearing are completely unfamiliar. And I have this underlying lost feeling, like I've woken up in someone else's life.

Was I in an accident? Do I have amnesia?

I start to breathe rapidly and I decide I need to get some air, immediately, before I pass out. I slam the laptop closed and grab the bag that was sitting at my feet, and ponytail-guy still doesn't look up as I run for the closest exit.

The air outside of the library is cool and the temperature is comfortable, but my surroundings are most certainly not. This place even smells totally foreign to me. My breath is still shallow and rapid, and my heart rate is steadily climbing, so I sit down on a ledge outside the building that is next to a giant pine tree. I rest my head in my hands and start to count, focusing on the sequential act and picturing the outline of each number in my mind. *One*, a long line down. *Two*, a detour and turn. *Three*, two more detours. *Four* right turns and I'm back again. I learned this technique from a counselor at NYU, back when I was fairly certain I was dying.

Chris ended things on a Thursday evening, and during the early hours of Friday morning, I tortured myself by watching the series finale of *E.R.* on my TiVo approximately five and a half times. When I finally stopped sobbing, I made that fateful call to Courtney and booked a flight back to Sunnyvale. It was all the money I had saved that semester, and I immediately panicked. I don't know whether it was the thought of returning home or the fact that I was now broke in Manhattan but the walls of my vision began caving in. My mind told my body that it either needed to flee the scene of danger or die. So I ran the four city blocks to the student health center and collapsed in the lobby. Any other health facility probably would've admitted me for psychiatric evaluation, but Theresa Lepore, impenetrable daughter of an Italian immigrant and seasoned counselor of spoiled rich kids, picked me up off the floor and told me to look directly into her dark Sicilian eyes. She told me slow down—to breathe in oxygen and out carbon dioxide, and then essentially to pull my shit together because my fears were not real.

Like that day, after several counting and slow breathing sessions, I'm able to gain some mental clarity and use it to steady myself enough to an upright position. Then, like Ms. Lepore instructed me, I make tangible, immediate goals.

I will get up. I will walk forward. I will find something familiar.

I pick up my laptop and stow it in the bag that I now discover contains a smart phone, a wallet, a few folders and pens, and a spiral notebook. I pull out the spiral first. The cover is a shiny blue cardstock with a gold emblem embossed on the front, that reads *UC Santa Cruz.* I open the notebook and leaf through the pages. Nearly every page contains my handwriting.

I slam it shut and look around. A young guy skateboards past me with a backpack. As my eyes follow him down the paved path away from the building, I scan the perimeter and see several more twenty-somethings either walking or biking along the intertwining foot paths. The dark asphalt contrasts against the vivid green of the manicured grass. Most are looking down at their smart phones and impressively maneuver themselves around hazards while still staring downward at the small handheld devices. I don't know what to do, or how I got here. I close my eyes and breathe in and out slowly for a few more minutes, counting to four over and over, and letting the oxygen disperse through my body. When I am slightly more calm, I pull out the wallet, looking for some hint of what the hell I'm doing here, on a college campus. On the West Coast. Alone. At least if I have some money I can get a cab—to who knows where.

I wipe my sweaty palms on the side of my jeans and open the wallet from the bag. I release my held breath when I realize there's some cash in it. I pull out some credit cards and set them aside and find a California driver's license. There I find the same terrible picture from when I was sixteen and, to the right of that, my parent's address in Sunnyvale. This is not surprising, since I never bothered to switch my ID to New York State until about a year or two ago. So I'm able to estimate my age is somewhere in the range of sixteen to twenty-five. But I still have no memory of this day of my life. Perhaps it was completely dull and inconsequential like most days I spent in northern California? If nothing remarkable happened to me, I likely just blocked the entire day out. I'm sure I'm just on a break from school and needed to escape my parents' house, so I made a trip to the library. I start to believe my inner monologue and the blood returns to my head, clearing out the fuzziness of panic and making room for more rational thought.

Something familiar. Something familiar.

I rummage around in the bag some more. The small interior pocket contains some mints, lip balm, and a receipt. The white paper is origamied into a tiny birdlike creature, so I unfold it. I can barely read the faded words but it appears to be from a coffee shop. I crush the small paper in my fist and run my clenched hand over my head, my long hair now dangling around my face as I rest my head on my knees. Through the ripped and frayed fabric of my jeans I notice something strange. My kneecap is completely smooth and blemishless. There's no scar.

With still very few clues about how I got here, I decide to look at the smart phone in my bag for my browsing history. It starts with rather unhelpful leads—several clothing websites with unprofessional attire, a few funny YouTube videos, and a podcast about staying true to yourself. I open Google Maps, and see that yesterday I had entered an address of a restaurant. Then, off to the side, I see another blue pin sticking there in the middle of downtown Santa Cruz. My heart pounds a deep resonating drum circle in my ear canal. I click on the little blue lollipop and I'm forced to read the name aloud to make myself believe it:

"Home."

39

MIKE

I fucking hate this part of the job. Tim and I sit behind his desk and this nineteen-year-old kid comes in, and we have to tell him to pack up and take off. But the part I hate the most is that this kid put his sweat, blood, and guts on the line for two weeks, and we don't even have the decency to sit him on the damn bench so that he can tell his dad he plays D1 lacrosse. This kid, like the others, is polite. He thanks us, and shakes our hands like a man, and then I get that tiny glimpse of the disappointment of a lifetime in his eyes as he looks towards the door.

"Well, that's that," Tim says to me as he moves some papers around on his desk.

I'm angry, but I can't show that to him. It's all part of the game. I pick up the stack of DVDs on the corner of his desk, and give him a nod, and make my way through the locker room hallway to the tape room. I stick the first one in and start jotting down notes about the Albany defense. But I'm distracted and I end up having to watch the first quarter twice.

After a little while, I stop the recording and cut the lights back on and rub my face between my hands. I decide I need to get out of here, and on the way home I swing by Breckenridge to have a beer to ease my frustration.

As I sit at the bar mindlessly slugging my pale ale and watching an old X-Games from God-knows when, a beautiful brunette bartender with giant fake tits steps in front of me to fill up some cups with the soda gun. I watch, unable to take my eyes off of her, as she turns around and pours two beers from the wall taps. I come here nearly every single week of the off-season, and I've never seen this gorgeous girl before. My eyes follow her back and forth as she gathers her tray of drinks and cocktail napkins and then she disappears into the back. I notice a tramp-stamp on the small sliver of skin between her shirt and shorts. I stare at the back exit that she left out of, willing her to come back, when another female voice breaks my concentration.

"Do you want another?"

I look up, somewhat startled from my trance, and there is a tall, slender blonde bartender looking at me expectantly. Her eyes are wide and kind and she smiles and blushes a little as I hold her gaze a little too long.

"You okay?" she says as she chuckles a little and wipes down the well. The stunning brunette returns with a case of beer, and the blonde one looks at me, knowingly.

"Her name's Brandi," she says casually as she continues cleaning.

"What? Who?" I say. Embarrassed, I look back down at my almost-empty beer glass, "Sure, I'll take one more—please," as I awkwardly hold it up and tilt the glass in her direction.

The blonde chuckles a little and her eyes meet mine again. I notice that they are a crazy deep blue-gray color. She turns around and I check out her ass as she fills my glass. It's nice—tight and not too small. I decide she's not hot but she's still attractive in a weird way. She turns around and catches me looking and chuckles again.

"Five bucks," she says as she puts the full glass in front of me.

I pass her my card and I decide to strike up a conversation, "You work here long?"

"Nah, just started Monday. Close it out?" she holds the card up as she asks.

"Yea, please."

She hands the card back to me and I just sit there like an idiot, drinking my beer and pretending to watch the TV. The blonde and brunette both crisscross back and forth in front of me several times, no doubt getting ready for the college rush later tonight. I can't help but watch them both, and inevitably I meet eyes with each a few times. I tell myself to stop being the creepy dude that's alone at the bar staring at women on a Thursday afternoon, but I can't help biology, man.

The brunette strikes up a conversation with an older patron down the bar, and my eyes are drawn back to the blonde, who is facing away from me again. I'm almost done with my beer, so I nurse it a little longer, enjoying the view. At least this has kept my mind off of all this lacrosse bullshit. The blonde turns slightly towards the wall and I see she's reading a book. She chews on her finger nails and taps her foot on the ground.

I smile, thinking, *I wonder what she is so engrossed in.*

I have a mild buzz and so I think of a brilliant plan to wave her over. She walks back over to stand in front of me, and I so charmingly ask if she knows of any good Mexican places nearby.

"I'm not really sure, I just moved here. But I can ask my manager if you want," she says innocently, and clearly without the faintest clue that I don't really care about the answer.

"No, no. That's okay. Thanks, though. I'm sure I'll figure something out," I get up and push my stool back under the bar. I shake my stiff knee out a little, grab my phone off the bar, and look her in the eyes again, "Hey, what's your name?"

"Jesse." And nothing else.

"Hey, Jesse, I'm Mike," I say while flashing her my most charming smile, "Maybe I'll catch you next time. I come here a lot after practice."

She bites, finally, "Practice? Are you in a band or something?" she asks without a hint of sarcasm.

I can't help but laugh, "No, I wish. I'm the assistant lacrosse coach at Denver."

"Oh, cool," she looks down at her feet and back at me, blushing again, "What's lacrosse?"

I smile and tell her that most people in Colorado don't know what lacrosse is, and I go into my whole mini-spiel about how it's the true American sport. She's nice, and listens attentively, unlike most girls I encounter at bars. But I keep losing my train of thought every time I look back up at her eyes. As I wrap up my canned explanation she smiles a sort-of half smile, and her sky eyes pierce through me.

"That sounds cool. I'd go see a game."

I smile again and write my number on the store copy of the receipt, and wave goodbye to her. I walk home to my apartment, the whole time trying to wipe the stupid grin off my face, as my phone vibrates in my pocket. I look at the screen and answer quickly.

"What's up shit-bag?" I laugh into the phone at Gavin.

I stop walking instantly and cover my eyes with my left hand. I listen.

After he's finished, and then after a few moments of silence, I speak, "I'm so sorry, man. I'm so sorry..."

40

KENDALL

I follow the little blue dot, which Google Maps claims is a nine-minute walk from my current location, and I'm fairly certain this is all just a strange mix-up. Looking up from the small screen, my destination appears as a dingy beige apartment building with weathered cedar shingles and a roof that looks like an original IHOP. I say little prayer to the universe that I don't actually live here and find solace in a shred of denial that's still lingering in my mind. That I must have somehow tapped into someone else's Google account on the campus WiFi.

I pace back and forth, from the building's entrance back to the curb and back again, and then circle the small patch of grass that appears to be some kind of courtyard. There's a small trash can, a bench, and some overgrown bushes. A crushed beer can rests next to the bench, my mind flicking back to the coffee table in Boulder and the sinking feeling of loss I can't seem to forget. Then I stand very still, trying to heighten my senses until anything looks, smells or feels familiar. A car drives by, and I watch it slow to a stop in a parking lot around the corner. A couple of surfers exit the car, hair wet and wetsuits pulled down to their waists. They look at me briefly with a small nod and grab their boards, heading towards a house. Their greeting is friendly but not one of recognition.

The rough idle of a small truck engine behind me grabs my attention and I look back towards the sound. A postal worker quickly shoves letters into the community mailbox across the way. I rush over to him before he can finish.

"Kendall Gibbons!—Please!" I shout to be heard over the truck.

The mailman looks at me like I'm crazy, but he looks down and shuffles through some stacks of letters, catalogs and small boxes. I hold out hope that he'll shrug at me in confusion when he comes up empty handed, but then, in seemingly slow motion, he holds out a stack of BOGO pizza coupons and credit card applications. I accept the pile, but I'm frozen and speechless. He gives me a strange look and puts the mail truck in drive, scooting away before he gets involved in whatever is ailing me. I look down, and the little window-pane of the top letter stares back at me with those familiar letters behind the thin plastic—

MS. KENDALL GIBBONS
234 FELIX ST, #2A
SANTA CRUZ, CA 95060

Without realizing it, I drop the mail in a pile at my feet and stare up at the faded building. Thankfully there is no one around to notice my internal crisis and inadvertent littering. All I can think is—*Gavin was right.*

My hands are shaking as I fumble through each key on my ring to find the right one. The door finally opens, and I step inside 2A. I take several deep breaths as I survey my surroundings. It's as old and crappy on the inside as it was on the outside, but the furnishings and decor do an adequate job of making it feel homey. There's a love-seat and a small TV on the wall in front of it, and a white coffee table that looks like it was made out of some kind of found driftwood. The walls are a bright, happy blue and all over it are photographs of beautiful places. The kitchen is a tiny corner of the room, with horrible avocado-colored tile and appliances, but there are blue and yellow accents that make it look kind of cute and retro. There is a tiny two-person table by a rather large window that lets in enough sunlight so that I don't need to flip on any lights. As I walk farther into the small space, I find a tiny room near the back of the apartment that holds a twin bed and nothing else, with a coral-colored curtain across the entrance. I walk back towards the kitchen, half expecting someone to come in and accuse me of breaking-and-entering. I look around and wander over to the sink to pour myself a glass of water. A photograph on the fridge suddenly catches my eye. I'm wearing a cap and gown, and Mike has his arm around my shoulders. We are both smiling ear to ear.

I drop the glass, and it shatters all over the floor.

After cleaning up my mess quickly with a dustpan I find under the sink, I return to the fridge to confirm the photo was indeed of me and my older brother. At second glance, I feel a strange mix of shock and relief. Next to the picture are some random magnets and a flyer for a book launch party. I scan past it as something catches my eye in the wording of the flyer—

SHORT STORIES by KENDALL GIBBONS.

I run over to a small desk that sits by the window and start rummaging through it. There is nothing but typical desk supplies, an old calculator, some envelopes, some paper clips. I sit down at the chair to think for a moment and then I grab the bag that contains the laptop. I pull up the browser and Google *www.manhattanfoodite.com* and immediately get a standard error message: "This webpage cannot be found."

Maybe it's the connection, I think, so I go to the browser homepage, and it loads instantly to the UC Santa Cruz Creative Writing website.

I am now having a full-fledge panic attack, and the walls of my vision are closing in around me. As the bright silver edges creep inwards, obscuring my peripheral vision, I try my blog URL again and get the same error. By this point I'm starting to black out, so I bend at the waist and put my head between my knees.

After a few minutes of sitting nearly upside down to keep blood flowing to my brain, my vision changes from spotty to just mildly hazy, and I decide to make my way over to the bed and lay down. It's not safe for me to be hyperventilating and nearly passing out in this unfamiliar apartment with no one around. I don't know what to do. Suddenly everything I knew to be true about myself seems to be drastically altered, and I don't even know how old I am or who I am. All I can think to do is try to find something, anything that's familiar and maybe that will calm me down so I can at least think straight.

I go over to the closet, which is basically just a rack in the back of the apartment and look at my clothes. I run my hands over the hangers and survey the contents. Gone are my wool pant suits, silk blouses, Tory Burch wedges, and Kate Spade tops. Gone is my favorite navy-blue blazer with the hot pink silk lining from J. Crew that I got to celebrate my first paid ad-space from Cuisinart. In its place are several pairs of worn-out jeans, flowy tops in earth tones, sandals, and a few dresses. There is no professional attire anywhere. I rummage faster and faster through the closet, tossing clothes wildly all over the bed and the floor, and nothing looks like mine. Then, at the bottom corner of the closet, resting on top of some shoe boxes, I see a familiar cartoon bear peeking back at me. I push a few sweaters aside and pull out the sweatshirt that reads *Boulder, Colorado* and I just start to fold into it and cry.

Everything has changed. And it's my fault.

—

At some point during my several hour freak-out session of tearing through all the items in the apartment in search of anything else that's familiar, I give in to my physical exhaustion and fall asleep on the bed amongst the T-shirts and old sweaters. I wake up an unknown amount of time later, startled by a strange song playing faintly from across the apartment. I look around for something to defend myself with against a possible music-carrying intruder, and I open the bedroom curtain. The small apartment is empty. The song lyric plays again, and then repeats a third time, and I realize it's a ring tone that's coming from a phone.

It plays a fourth time, and I suspect that I should answer it. I pick it up, and see *MOM* lit up in blue on the screen. I slide the little button and put her on speaker-phone.

"Hello?" I say weakly, uncertain if I'd even recognize my own voice.

"Oh, Kendall, I'm sorry—I didn't mean to wake you."

"Mom?"

"Yes, sweetie, I'm so sorry to call so early but your brother's on his way here and we need to borrow your old Bible. The one that Grandma Gibbons gave you? Do you know where you may have stuck it?"

I pause, trying to digest the past several hours and answer her question, "What? Mike's on his way there? What? Why does he need a Bible?"

She exhales, softly muffling the phone for a beat, "Oh sweetie, Mikey's gotta read a Bible verse today at the funeral."

"Funeral? Who's funeral? — Someone died?" I sit cross-legged on the small living room floor and twist my hair around my ring finger nervously.

She pauses for a moment, and continues in a much lower, quieter voice, "I'm sorry I thought Mike would've told you honey, Gavin's mom passed away on Wednesday night. The service is in a few hours."

After a very long moment of silence, my mom asks me if I am still on the line.

"Ya—yeah—I'm here."

"Do you remember where you may've put it?"

I flatly give her my best guess.

"Oh, wonderful. Thank you so much. Well, I've gotta go help your father find his black suit-pants, so I'll call you back later tonight."

"Oh-kay. Bye Mom."

I put the phone down on the carpet and stare at it. I know that this day had come and gone before, but now it's different. I am invested in it. And I couldn't stop it.

I lay on the carpet staring up at the ceiling, and all I can think about are those damn brown eyes. All their hope, all their life, extinguished in an instant. The ugly popcorn ceiling becomes a blur of white as my eyes fill with tears. But I don't move; I don't sob audibly. It's like I just leak from deep inside and lay there helpless to stop it. I've cried after injuries, or even after my own heartbreak all those years ago, but I've never cried like this. I can't think about the past few hours of confusion and complete transformation, or about Manhattan, or my brother. All I can think about is the gaping hole in Gavin's heart and how I would give anything to fill it.

I don't know what to do, or who to be right now. The old me wouldn't even have known about this until months from now, nor would she even really have cared. If it would stop this feeling I have right now, maybe my life was better off disconnected like that? If I jump in my car, and I get back in that elevator, maybe I can go backwards in time again and run like hell away from Gavin and Mike. Part of me wants that more than anything, even more than I ever wanted to meet Susan Wilder. But the other part of me, the glutton-for-punishment that seems to be growing stronger and stronger every day, wants to feel more instead of less. To feel happy and exhausted like after snowboarding all day, to feel scared like when Gavin reached for my elbow, to feel stillness like when I walked through Boulder alone, to feel powerful like when I sprayed that douchebag in the face and got us the hell out of there. When I was in New York, alone and determined to be someone I never really was, I didn't feel anything.

So, against my better judgment, I let my newfound feelings guide me to the car, start the ignition, and drive the forty-five minutes back to Sunnyvale. I drive in silence, trying to think of anything worthwhile to say to him, but I come up with nothing.

41

MIKE

The inside of the church is brick with vaulted ceilings. Behind me, there's a huge window in the shape of a cross, spreading from floor to ceiling, the seams of glass fragments sewn together to give it a purposefully shattered look. Looking through it, the sky and trees beyond are kaleidoscoped into a million pieces.

I stand under the bright church lights, in between flower arrangements, staring at a group of people who would rather be anywhere but here. They came because they had to—because Mrs. Bennett meant something to them or impacted them during her relatively brief time on this planet. I wait for the music to stop before I start to read the verse she picked out. I have a lump in my throat thinking about how freaking scary it must be to know you're going to die.

I clear my throat and begin, "To every thing there is a season, and a time to every purpose under the heaven: A time to be born, and a time to die; a time to plant, a time to reap that which is planted; A time to kill, and a time to heal; a time to break down, and a time to build up; A time to weep, and a time to laugh; a time to mourn, and a time to dance; A time to cast away stones, and a time to gather stones together; a time to embrace, and a time to refrain from embracing; A time to get, and a time to lose; a time to keep, and a time to cast away; A time to rend, and a time to sew; a time to keep silence, and a time to speak; A time to love, and a time to hate; a time of war, and a time of peace."

42

KENDALL

I pull my car into the church parking lot and am confronted by an onslaught of memories. This is the building where I spent nearly every Sunday (and a lot of forced Wednesday and Friday nights) of my young life. Seeing something I tried to forget for so long, I am ironically comforted by the familiarity of the brick and glass—the strange club that claims to be open to everyone but yet is so foreboding that no one would just show up. I still have a memory of this part of my old life.

Glancing down at my watch, I'm late, as I suspected I would be after changing five times and then struggling to locate my car in the apartment parking lot. The obituary said the service was supposed to start twenty minutes ago. I make the decision to stay put until people start filing out and then make my way in to pay my respects.

I sit in the car in silence and try to talk myself into leaving. Reason number one to leave: my attire. Since my hippie closet had minimal formal attire, and absolutely none of it was black, I chose a dark blue dress with a reverse cowl neck that hangs down to the middle of my back. I was in a hurry, so I didn't have time to do anything with my long, wavy brown hair so I just twisted it up in a messy bun. I now decide to let the bun out, and my hair cascades down my shoulders, almost covering my entire back in silky brown waves. Nervously I put a little more makeup on to kill some time, and looking at myself now, I actually feel kind of pretty. I then internally scold myself for being so vain at a time like this and slam the visor mirror closed while I immediately push these ridiculous thoughts out of my head. I am so uneasy that each minute that advances on my dashboard clock feels like ten.

Reason number two: risk of running into my parents. Though I've been in much more contact recently with my mother than ever before, I still risk being emptied by one disappointed look, one critical comment. I'm not sure which version of Kendall they will know- the one who stopped caring about those things out of self-preservation or the one who is now newly vulnerable to them. The magnetic force that pulled me back here makes that uncertainty tolerable for once. I have to just see him, if only for a second.

After the minutes continue to creep by, a few middle-aged couples begin slowly filtering out of the church doors and into the parking lot. All of their expressions are similar—that of shock, exhaustion, and ambivalence. The sun is a blasphemous ray, making a mockery of everyone's grief with its beauty. Jokes and laughter are unimaginable. But so are silly reservations.

I look through my dingy windshield, and after at least several dozen people have left, I get out of the car and walk slowly towards the church entrance. I pull the heavy wooden door open, and enter, making sure to catch the door behind me so that it doesn't slam and call unneeded attention my way. There are a few groups of people standing around talking in hushed voices, off to the sides of the pews. There is a large floral arrangement near the pulpit and thankfully a small urn instead of a casket. At the sight of it, I let my breath out slowly; realizing for the first time that I've been holding it. I stand for a moment in the back of the church, the smell of the old building wafting memories over me like a dam giving way.

I scan around the room, and over in the corner, I see my brother talking with some older adults, most of whom are obscured from my view by a large pillar. He looks so grown-up in his suit and tie, and stands like a man, with his chest forward and shoulders back. I move towards the left side of the church, around the back side of the pews, and now I can see the rest of the group that he's talking to. In addition to two older couples, no doubt from our parents' church circle, there's a tall, attractive blond woman, probably in her twenties, who's dressed impeccably and hanging on Mike's every word. She looks so familiar that I can't take my eyes off of her, and as I get closer—I realize why. The last time I saw her, she was loading up on eyeliner and drunkenly ending up in a compromised position with a total stranger.

Luckily Courtney and my brother are too engrossed in conversation to notice me in the back of the church, because I'm sure I look insane with my intense, mouth-agape stare. I'm frozen in place as I watch Courtney place a hand on my brothers arm and whisper something in his ear. She then leaves the group and makes her way over to the other side of the pulpit. She approaches a tall, muscular man who is facing away from me. From the back all I can see is his chestnut brown wavy but short hair and confident stance leaning on one leg. She wraps her arms around his waist, and as he turns his head and plants a kiss on the top of her head, I have to stop myself from audibly screaming.

I debate turning around, running back to my car, and driving as far away from here as I can possibly get. But I can't take my eyes off of him. And her. Them. *Together.*

I stand in the back of the church, completely still and staring at my ex-best friend with her arm around Gavin's waist, and my face feels like it's suddenly on fire. I'm dizzy and I start to shuffle slowly backwards to get my bearings and find something to lean against, when I bump into someone.

"Excuse me," I hear a familiar voice behind me whisper apologetically to me. I wheel around and come face-to-face with my mother. Without thinking I clobber her with a hug and bite my lip to keep from crying. She smells and feels so comforting that for a moment I almost forget the shocking image of Gavin and Courtney together.

"Kendall?" she says, obviously shocked to see me, "Are you okay?"

She pulls back to look at my face and her face is full of concern, but I can also tell she is drained, no doubt from mourning her friend. I feel an urge to make her feel better, and so I lie, "Yeah, I'm okay," I force a slight smile, "I came to check on you. How are you holding up?"

"Oh, well—we're okay. It's a terrible tragedy, but she was suffering. Now she's in peace," my mom's eyes shine with newly forming tears, but she looks away and wipes them off quickly, pausing for a few beats before continuing, "I just hate to think that she won't be able to see Gavin become a husband and father—she would've been a wonderful grandmother."

"What? Is he—getting married?" I ask, trying to stifle my tone of part shock and part devastation.

"No, no honey. I just mean some day," she looks at me with a hint of suspicion in her eyes.

I look down at my feet and try to change the subject away from Gavin, "Where's Dad?"

"He drove ahead to the grave site. He's helping with the arrangements," she wrings her hands as she talks and looks over my shoulder towards the urn that sits at the front of the church, next to the piano.

We are fairly far away, but I see now that there are pictures on top of the piano of Gavin and Mr. and Mrs. Bennett. The pulpit groups have now dissipated, and there are only a few final stragglers left in the chapel. I decide it's safe to walk up to the front to say my goodbye. As I advance up the aisle, I reflect on the fact that I came here with mixed intentions—I wanted to see Gavin, but I also selfishly wanted to gauge his reaction to seeing me. Now, much like the present, my plan is completely flipped on its head. I don't care about any of that crap anymore—I just want to make her come back to life. To go back in time before Courtney and he found each other. To tell him I love him. To do more than just bury a few cartons of cigarettes. I step up to the urn and say a silent prayer for Gavin's mother, and wish with all of my being that I could have done more.

I look back and the church is now almost empty. My mom remains, picking up stray prayer cards from the pews near the middle of the row. I decide to help her and start cleaning up the first few rows, but I'm horribly slow because I can't stop looking back at the urn and thinking about how the woman who was so sweet and kind to me as a little girl is gone. Her earthly state is reduced to the small contents of that vessel. She should have this ability to bounce around time—not me.

As I stare at the urn, my mind drifts to the last time I saw her—to the care and attention she received from her son. The little happy, brown-eyed boy with a fishing pole that looked back at me from her dresser a few days ago, now peeks out at me again from a small, gold frame behind a vase of purple lilies. I'm again drawn to the photograph of pure innocence and joy. And at this moment, here in this church from my childhood, I can't help but feel the opposite of that little brown-eyed boy—completely and utterly lost.

A thump behind me jolts me back. I turn and my mom has dropped a box on the front pew.

"Can you help me get everything together? We have to take the photos over to the house for the reception."

"Sure," I say as I pick up my favorite photo and wrap it in the old, crumpled tissue paper from the box. It smells like moth balls and cedar. *Like home,* I think. I pick up the vase of lilies, and as I turn to my right, I ask, "Mom, what do you want me to do w—"

I stop mid-question and realize that my mom has already returned to the back of the church, busying herself with more tasks. The figure that's now occupying my mother's previous space steps closer, and I look up into his kind eyes, holding the flowers awkwardly, "W—with these?"

"Hey," he says quietly and warmly.

"Hi Gavin," I respond, still staring dumbly up at him.

"You can keep those."

When I am silent in response, he explains, "There are a ton more in the backyard," he doesn't break eye contact with me right away. "They were my mom's favorite, so I planted a whole bed of them outside her window a few months ago."

I did not know a human heart could feel like it was aching with each individual beat. I try to speak, but nothing will come out of my mouth. I feel a single tear flow down my right cheek, but Gavin does not notice as he starts helping wrap up the picture frames. I don't know why, but my arm is drawn towards his shoulder. I place my hand on it and squeeze gently, and Gavin turns towards me, confused.

"I—I'm so sorry," I say desperately, pulling my arm back quickly and hugging it to my chest.

Gavin looks at me and offers a small nod in reply. I take a second to look back at him, his face tanned lightly and his face clean-shaven. And I can finally see him. He is one of the most handsome men I have ever seen in real life, with a chiseled jaw, strong nose, and black eyelashes lining his currently copper eyes. And there is something new in them that I can't pinpoint. It's like a strange conflict of disappointment and hope. We both look away after lingering for too long and continue to pack the box in silence.

When we're done, I grab the vase of flowers again and follow him out into the parking lot. I pull the flowers out of the vase and dump the water onto the asphalt. I use the edge of my dress to wipe the water off of the glass and hand the empty vase to Gavin to add to the box. He takes it and pauses, and then looks down at me. Our eyes lock again and I can't think.

"Thanks," he says sincerely, holding my gaze. My stomach flutters—my mind complete mush. "I guess I'll see you later," he says, opening the door to the driver's seat.

Desperate to keep him from leaving, I quickly ask, "Are you going back to Boulder soon?"

"Actually I moved back in with my pare—," he pauses a beat, "—my dad. Just temporarily."

I see the pain return to his eyes and think back to a few days ago when he helped me down the mountain. He was so patient with me and so kind. Why can't I be that way?

"Well, maybe we can meet up soon—go back to that place you took me—must've been two years ago? The one with the good live music and tables outside? We can finally get a beer and catch up," I say quickly, hoping that he doesn't notice that my voice is wobbling with nervousness and uncertainty about the past.

"You mean when you blew me off?" he says, finally cracking a half-smile.

"I think you were the one that left," I say, smiling back at him in relief that he remembers, that it actually happened and not just in my memory, "not that I don't blame you."

"Yah, you were kinda a bitch," he says, laughing and flinching as I pretend to hit his arm.

"You can bring Courtney," I say, looking off to the side, trying not to be obvious.

He laughs, "I don't know—she hates beer."

I smile again and tell him I guess not much has changed. Courtney was always the girlier of the two of us, and her preferences in beverages reflected that. I distinctly remember an obsession she had with whip-cream vodka—that vile syrupy chemical masquerading as a good way to make young girls interested in an old Russian man's drink. Most of me is now equally as disgusted at the idea of Courtney and Gavin as a couple.

After her summer of excitement in LA, Courtney would constantly reassure me that she was still my best friend, and we were going to be each other's maids-of-honor in our future weddings, but I could see the doubt seeping in. Just like my parents and my older brother, she was disappointed in me. And so I fulfilled that new role of shitty best friend rather than invisible best friend. I told my parents she was there that night with the Asshole, that she encouraged my bad choices, when the truth of it was she was the one who tried everything she could to protect me. They forbid me from having her at the house, from mentioning her name. And so after that our bestie status was no longer. I wasn't even woman-enough to end it myself. So there is a small part of me, as a newly enlightened twenty-three-year-old, that now feels like Karma is a bitch. I had my chance, or chances. I blew it.

We stand there a few seconds and I say goodbye, both of us hesitating to leave.

My internal struggle gives way and the small part of me that doesn't care what anyone thinks reaches out to hug Gavin around the waist. I bury my head in his shoulder and give him a solid, heartfelt squeeze. I pull him as close as I can and his smell overwhelms me and calms me at the same time. I feel his body tense from surprise and then slowly relax into the hug, finally resting his cheek against the top of my head. It takes all of my willpower to pull away, and I look up at him, probably noticeably flustered.

"Bye Gavin."

"Bye Kendall."

I walk back to my car with absolutely no idea of where I'm going, but certain about where I would rather be.

43

KENDALL

I don't want to be alone again in that unfamiliar apartment so I drive the few miles that are burned into my brain. I pull into my parent's driveway and unlock the side door. Everything looks exactly as I left it just a few days ago, but this time it is eerily silent in my childhood home.

My mind starts recounting each day of this crazy journey, and I'm overwhelmed and saddened by how small I am in the concept of time. I couldn't change anything when I actually wanted to—I just made different mistakes the second time around. And now I don't recognize my life at all. I curl into a ball on my mother's couch and cover my head with a pillow. All I can think about is how much I want to talk to Gavin, or even to just share the same space, the same air. I don't care if I'm twenty-three, fifteen, eight or ninety. I don't care if anyone reads my freaking non-sense about prosciutto and cheese and wine pairings. Who gives a fuck about food that much anyway?

I've spent the better part of the last twelve hours crying and/or feeling like my insides were being unhinged and pulled in multiple directions. And my life has been drastically altered from what I always thought I wanted.

Someone I loved has died, and though I've forgotten about living, I am not dead. This thought pulls me up from the fetal position, and I stand in the center of the living room. I look around at the familiar furniture in the room, and the pictures on the wall. I look down at my legs, my bare feet, and the floor under them. I turn towards the door, swing it open, and just run. The pavement is harsh and rough under my bare feet, but I continue running until the street ends. I run through the field, and then through the stream. My legs are burning, but I don't stop. I run through the patch of woods and up the hill to the clearing. My heart pounds in my ears as I slow to a walk in the cool, damp grass. I let my body fall to the earth and I just lay silently under the sky. The sun is beginning to dip below the tree line that surrounds me, casting long shadows over my spread arms. I hear only quiet hums of insects and wind against the leaves.

I lay still until the sun dips low enough to cast a blue tint over everything. I slowly rise from the ground and walk towards the path that led me here, leaving from the veil I hid behind for so long.

—

When I quietly enter the house, the warm glow of a lamp is the only light illuminating the living room. In the far corner, my brother is asleep in a chair, still in his suit, with only his tie loosened a bit.

I walk over and gently nudge his shoulder, and he opens his eyes briefly and shifts his weight, resting his head on his hand and closing his eyes again.

"Hey," he says sleepily, "what time is it?"

"I'm not sure," I respond, and I decide to sit on the floor a few feet from him.

He rubs his face and I notice his hands have aged since I last saw him. They are the hands of a man, strong and weathered.

"I met someone."

I look at him and pause, shocked at the intimacy of the conversation he chose to initiate with me. I hesitate to ask too much too fast.

"She's different—she's...real," he smiles, and looks me in the eye, like this is a totally normal conversation for us.

Maybe it is, I think. I wait for him to continue, trying not to looked stunned.

"I'm trying not to fuck it up."

"What do you mean?"

"You know, not act too eager but also eager enough. The fucking dance."

"Yea," I pretend to know what he's talking about. I haven't exactly been the queen of interpersonal relationships for the past eight to ten years.

"I wasn't going to text her tonight, because of the funeral and all that, but I couldn't help myself," he smiles like he's trying not to, "she makes everything clearer."

We talk about this girl for a while, and then about his disappointments with his job right now. I discover that Mike has found a career that he's passionate about, and I realize for the first time 'what my cup runneth over' means. Even in all my small successes with my blog, I never felt this overwhelming sense of pride that I do now. I just want to keep talking to Mike all night and hear how he thinks coaching could be so much more without the business aspect of athletics. I want to hear about his triumphs and his failures, and how Jesse, his new girlfriend, makes him laugh without even trying. After he's finished talking, we sit in comfortable silence and my eyes start to feel heavy. As I struggle to keep them open, I can tell he's deep in thought. I interrupt by taking a chance,

"Mike, I'm really lucky to be your sister," I say earnestly.

"I know," he says, straight-faced.

I hit him with a pillow and he laughs and we say goodnight and head up to our childhood bedrooms like we did so many other nights before. I stay up writing for as long as I can keep my eyes open and fall asleep suddenly and unexpectedly on my journal.

44

MIKE

"What does that even mean? 'a time to every purpose'?"

"Why are you analyzing the Bible, man?"

"Your mom knew. She totally knew."

"Knew what?"

"That time is not really linear. Time just gives our minds context for all the before and after."

"Lay off the weed, Mikey," Gavin laughs at me.

"I'm serious. Remember that night?"

"Of course I remember"

"Then you know. Like she knew."

Gavin pauses. "Alright I gotta go break up with Courtney."

"What?" I say, hitting speakerphone and waving Jesse over to listen.

"Courtney. I can't bullshit her anymore. She's hot and all, but, she's not it."

Jesse furrows her brow and pushes me away from her, putting her hands over her ears and shaking her head dramatically.

I take Gavin off speakerphone, smiling at her smugly and putting my phone back up to my ear, "I had a feeling."

"What does that mean?"

"Dude, nothing. I just know you better than anyone. And I knew you weren't ever that into her."

"Fair enough."
"When you coming back around these parts?"
"Dunno. I'll hit you up tomorrow though. I gotta go."

After my celebration dance, Jesse and I get in the car and head out to a late dinner, and I hate the ride there because I have to drive instead of stare at her. Every time I see her she just gets hotter. We meet eyes several times and she laughs, asking me about Gavin and Courtney and why they weren't a good fit.

"He's just confused."

"Confused about what?"

"I don't know. Life? I guess he felt like he needed to show his mom he was okay."

"So, he got a girlfriend for his mom?"

"Sort of. Gavin's weird. He never really dated any girls for longer than a few weeks. I've always thought he was holding out for someone in particular."

"Who?"

"My sister," I laugh.

"Really? Does that piss you off?"

"It used to. Now nothing really pisses me off."

"What do you mean?"

"I have everything I ever wanted. Why would I be pissed off?" I grin.

She smiles at me and interlaces her fingers with mine. I pull into a parking spot behind the restaurant and cut the engine, and as I'm unbuckling my seatbelt, she dives over the center console and kisses me, pulling herself into a kneeling position over my seat so that she's straddling me. My hands find her waist, her back, pulling her against me as my heart pounds and my body reacts to everything about her. She pulls back, smiling at me, breathless and beautiful with the dim parking lot light behind her.

"Third date and I'm not a slut, right?"

"You're such a slut."

"Shut up Gibbons."

And just like that, one of my adolescent dreams has come to fruition.

—

We decide to skip the restaurant altogether and get burgers and milkshakes at a nearby drive-thru. We park up on the hill where Gavin brought me after my injury, and we eat our food on the front hood of my car, talking and laughing. This spot has become a sort of refuge for me when life gets too heavy to handle.

After I blew out my knee, I drank myself into oblivion for a while, and made some terrible decisions. But it was my sister who never gave up on me. We didn't speak much to each other but she wrote me long letters—some about nothing in particular, some about the past, and most about my future. Which was a dim light at the end of the train tunnel that had been fading quickly into the distance as I sprinted away from it.

"So tell me about your family," Jesse says, laying her head back into the crook of my arm, looking up into the empty clouds that obscure the millions of stars behind them.

"What about them?"

"I don't know—what are they like? Are they like you?"

"No," I laugh, "not really."

"Can I meet them?"

This question normally would be a red flag for a stage-five clinger—but when it comes from Jesse it doesn't sound like that. It sounds like something I think I want too.

"Well, you met Gavin. He's family."

"Of course. But your parents?"

"My parents are kinda nuts, but sure, you can meet them."

"What about your sister?"

"She's even nuttier."

Jesse laughs and rolls so she's facing towards me. She kisses me and then buries her face into my chest, closing her eyes.

"Why do you want to know all of this?"

She pauses, and then smiles, "Guess."

"Because you think I'm the Golden State Killer?"

"Duh."

This time I laugh and she rises to her knees and hovers over me, pinning my arms to the hood of the car next to me, attempting to hold me down with her entire body weight. I use my legs and wrap them around her torso and she falls onto me. We both laugh until we are breathless, and then lay with our legs intertwined, her head on my chest.

"My sister's great. She's kind of an old soul."

Jesse lays quietly, letting me continue, "Ever since we were in high school, she has been looking out for me. And I'm the older brother—it's supposed to be reversed. But she just seemed to understand life a lot sooner than the rest of us."

"What do you mean?"

"Well, she just didn't need to live by anyone else's rules."

"I'm jealous."

"Yea, me too. I guess a near-death experience will do that to you."

"What?" Jesse perks up.

"When we were in high school, we think she was electrocuted in an elevator after a power surge. No one really knows but she's never been the same since."

"That's insane. Was she okay after? Like physically?"

"Yea the emergency room doctors said there was zero evidence of any injuries, but she lost consciousness for a while. They never could explain it."

"Weird!" Jesse says, her hand covering her mouth in shock.

"Yea, and I think Gavin has been fascinated by her ever since. Like he thinks she's some kind of super hero."

KENDALL

The wind catches my hair and whips it around my face, obscuring my view of the distant parking lots and streets and rooftops below. The sun is setting on San Jose, and the working crowd is departing. A few street lights are coming on, and the hum of the small city sounds like the last goodbyes of a party, the faint murmur of cars and buses drifting away into the distance. On the other side, the distant purple-blue of the mountains feels like a fake backdrop in a movie. I look down at the ground below and feel a nervousness and a rush of adrenaline. I lean over the concrete ledge and close my eyes, feeling the wind against my skin and the last of the sun's rays against my face. Then I lean back toward the roof of this building I've come to know very well from the inside. Once again, I'm back here.

After I woke up in my childhood bedroom, and Mike was already gone, I spent the day hulled up and writing. But this time I was writing a letter. To Courtney.

> *Courtney,*
>
> *You are a beautiful person and a great friend. I'm sorry I didn't tell you this enough, but I cherish the memories of our silliness and creativity that helped define me. Thank you for realizing what I needed when I had no clue. I hope that you can do the same for Gavin as he wades, drifts and tumbles through these stages of grief. I can tell you both from experience that time truly does heal our deepest scars and that people don't leave you behind unless you let them. So hold onto each other for dear life.*
>
> *And—it really should be very simple—just be yourself, and all you really need is love to get you there. I'm sorry for all the memories lost between us before I stumbled upon this truth.*
>
> *Much love and bye, bye,*
>
> *Bye,*

Kendall

After I put the letter in her parents' mailbox, I drove around Sunnyvale and watched life happening. There were people driving, going to the bank, getting sandwiches, talking, arguing, playing on their phones, getting their car washed, and just going through the mundane moments of everyday life. But these snapshots were also full of moments that were anything but mundane. A friendly smile, a hug between friends, a baby's belly laugh at her father, and a spontaneous dance party in a passing car. It would be inaccurate to state that these moments make life complete, because this implies there is a finish line or a resolution. Rather, these moments simply make life full. And my mistake all these years was trying to save some room for the future.

And now I'm back here, and I can't believe I'm about to get in a metal box and travel through time to an unknown destination. On purpose.

I open the heavy metal door back into the building's interior and it slams behind me, echoing down the stairwell. I descend a half flight of stairs and go through a door marked *Emergency Exit Only* on the opposite side, heading for the twenty-eighth-floor elevator bank. I feel calm and ready. I press the down button and wait for the ding.

45

YEAR 28(B)

KENDALL

A woman's voice awakens me very suddenly from a deep sleep, and I find myself on a plush, white couch with a pale blue blanket draped over me. The sun is coming up through a window across the room, the pale blue light gradually lightening my surroundings. After rubbing my eyes and sitting up a bit, I realize the woman's voice is coming from the TV that rests on a large console table in this very strange living room. It's a familiar morning news program—one that was on in the background during breakfast almost every morning before school. But the woman that is speaking is not the typical host, and her voice draws me into the program but I'm not sure why. It's a cooking segment, so the camera is focused on her hands, which are whipping cream into soft, perfect peaks in a silver bowl. Then, as the camera cuts from her hands back up to her face, I realize why I recognized the voice: it's Susan Wilder.

I watch until the end of the segment, and then the host wraps up with some very personal questions aimed at Ms. Wilder. She takes them in stride, smiling ear to ear and answering vaguely and confidently.

"You know, Bill, my philosophy in life is the same as my philosophy in the kitchen—start with flawless ingredients, set the bar high, and hire someone else to wash the dishes afterward."

The television personalities laugh over-enthusiastically at her clever metaphor and the program cuts to commercial.

I rise from the couch, and move towards the large living room window, still clutching the blanket to my chest. As I approach it, my vantage point moves from a cloud-scattered sky to an expansive view of the ocean. I am frozen in place, half from surprise and half because I am hypnotized by the beauty of it. The noise from the TV fades out of my consciousness, and I stare out at the horizon, filled with an odd sensation. I can only think of one word to describe it: Peace.

I stretch my arms up towards the ceiling and have an urge to smell, taste and hear the ocean, so I look for a window that opens, and stick my head out into the sea air. I sit there, hanging out the window and laughing at this ridiculous moment when I am suddenly aware that I am acutely alone. I'm not sad about this but realize that the moment might be somewhat incomplete.

I leave the window open and pull myself back into the apartment, which is beautiful and simple and clean. I look at the pictures on the wall and see my family smiling back at me. I can't help but reach out and touch the framed photographs to make sure they're real. My heart swells like the sea beneath me. This place, like the other apartment, does not spark any memories of my past, but this time, I feel like somethings familiar. I can't pinpoint exactly what it is, but it leaves me feeling calm instead of panicked and afraid of the unknown.

I make my way to the kitchen, in search of coffee. When I survey the pictures on the hallway wall, I realize they are of Mike and I chronologically, all the way from infancy to adulthood. The final picture in this sequential hall is of Mike is taken at a restaurant, Mike sitting at a table, grinning, with his arm around a very cute blond. Then across the hall is a strange collage of my parents on what appears to be a cruise.

I move into the kitchen, where I find my grandmother's tea towels placed over the oven handle in perfect order. As a kid, I would constantly wipe my hands on them, leaving them damp and in disarray. And then I would return to the kitchen later and find them neatly folded and back in place.

"Mom?" I call back towards the hallway. *Silence.*

"Dad?"

Still no response. I make my way through the remaining rooms. There's a small bedroom with twin beds and flamingo sheets, pale pink walls, and a sign that says *The beach is my happy place.* The room looks immaculate and untouched.

The next room on the right appears to be the master bedroom with a large four-post bed and white linens. There is a large dark wood dresser with photos of my parents in various frames. They look happy and carefree, words that just a few weeks ago I would never have used in their vicinity. I sit on the edge of their bed and look down at my hands. They are still my hands- with slightly too-short fingers and knobby knuckles that I inherited from my dad. They haven't changed.

I step into the master bathroom and flip on the light to inspect my appearance. I must be older, with a few tiny fine lines around my eyes and any trace of baby fat gone from my cheeks, but my hair is still brown and long, with subtle golden highlights, and falls well beyond my shoulders. My face is tan, and there are clumps of mascara under my eyes. I clearly slept in my makeup, so I start to wipe it off with a tissue. My appearance is not as indicative of my exact age as I was hoping. I can only really estimate I'm in my mid-to-late twenties, so I search the apartment for a computer to verify the date. There's a desktop in what appears to be an office, so I power it up. In the bottom right corner, I find the date:

September 26, 2016.

It's been two weeks since I walked into that elevator to see Ms. Wilder. My hair is different, my clothes are different, and I'm in a strange apartment near the ocean, but I'm finally twenty-eight again.

Before the shock and elation begin to sink in, a smart phone vibrates against the bedside table and lights up *MIKE FaceTime call.* I rush to answer it, desperate for answers to so many questions. The screen goes from blank to full of smiling faces, and I recognize three of the four.

They all exclaim happily, in unison, almost like they practiced it beforehand, "Hi Kendall!"

Silly laughter follows from my mother, father, and brother. They all look positively giddy, and so I smile and wave, trying to act like I know this fourth person, a petite and pretty blonde.

Is she the one from the wall photo?

As if she could hear my thoughts, she smiles knowingly and holds up her left hand.

"Jesse and I got engaged last night!" Mike announces, taking her hand and kissing it. Everyone giggles with glee again and my dad pats Mike on the shoulder.

I'm silent until I realize they're all looking at me, waiting for a response. I put on my best happy face and smile at them, "Congratulations guys!"

They all react again by cheering. My mom hugs the girl called Jesse that is now Mike's fiancé, and there is a shuffle of indistinct sounds and images on the screen as Mike takes the phone into the other room so it's just him and I.

"Ken, the plan worked perfectly—thanks for all your help," his voice lowered.

"Oh—great! I'm so glad!" I do my best to sound authentic, though I'm thoroughly confused.

"Jesse's really excited to see you tomorrow, too. She'll have someone to talk to about all this wedding-shit," he says out of the side of his mouth, looking back towards the direction he came from and then winking at me.

I keep a smile plastered to my face and nod, trying not to look surprised.

See her tomorrow?

"Thanks again, Ken. We love you."

My heart aches and swells with those three words. My brother has never said them to me before.

"Love you too," I say, trying to bite my lip to keep it from noticeably quivering.

"Alright, gotta go. See you at the airport."

The screen goes blank and my eyes well up with tears. I rub them and take deep breaths until I start to feel myself calm down a little bit.

"Get it together, Kendall," I say audibly, hoping it will influence me more than simply a thought.

Dying to find out what Mike meant, I scroll through my inbox and find my flight confirmation— I leave at five-thirty AM for Denver.

46

MIKE

As I pack up the last of my belongings, I look around the half-empty room and can't help but feel a little bit nostalgic about this shit-hole of an apartment. After Gavin moved out and Jesse and I got serious, it was certainly a lot cleaner and less frequently reeked of pot, but it still represented my independence and, in a small way, my success. I pull out my old, ratty poncho from a box that says *DONATIONS* and pull it over my head.

I put my hands in the front pocket and feel a crumpled piece of paper. I pull it out and unfold it, and at first I don't recognize the handwriting. I start reading the first few lines.

> *His limp from wounds of battles lost, of dreams shattered into the wind;*
> *He lies lifeless most days, without a thought of what might become.*

I think I remember these words, as heat rises to my face—more out of embarrassment than anger.

I scoop him up and fly him over the mountains,
Into the elevator and back in time
He is running, jumping, springing back to life

These are my sister's words. Almost ten years ago.

I continue reading:

Well, that was my attempt at poetry and it neither rhymed nor was it coherent. But I do feel like I've been granted this strange and seemingly never-ending journey for a reason now—to help Mike. I know he has it in him to be whatever he wants to be. And when he's done hating me and hating himself, hopefully I can help him see that. All this time I've been rushing to get back to my life in New York, and it was never really a life. So I've decided something— I'll stay here as long as I need to to get my brother back.

All those years ago and turns out my little sister was wiser than me. And still is. My stomach pangs with an empty feeling that I can only describe as regret. I remember how I treated her that day, and how much worse it could have been if Gavin hadn't been there. I hold her words in my right hand and rub my forehead with my left, thinking about how much has changed since that day. I suddenly feel warm arms around my shoulders and sweet breath on my neck.

"Whatcha looking at?" Jesse whispers in my ear, kissing me lightly just below it.

My hand instinctively falls to her arm, which is draped over my chest from behind.

"Found this old letter-thing. Kendall wrote it a long time ago."

"What's it about?"

"How she wanted to save me."

"What?"

"You know, back when I'd just hurt my knee. I was really fucked up."

"So she wrote you a letter?"

"Well...sort of. I was drunk and read her journal and it was about me."

Jesse shoves my head to the side with her hand and laughs, "Asshole! You read your sister's journal?"

I laugh with her and grab her wrists as she playfully tries to pull away from me.

"I'm not sure I can marry a man that could do something so dishonest," she says, with a flirtatious glimmer in her eye, "and to your sweet sister nonetheless."

"Oh, c'mon, I was twenty-one and drunk and pissed off at the world. Times have changed. And she wasn't always so sweet," I pull her down, so she's sitting on my lap. I run my hand lightly over her arm, and she picks up the crumpled pages.

"So, did you save this?"

"I don't remember—I just remember not being able to throw it away."

Jesse looks at me knowingly and kisses the top of my head. She grabs a box and heads back to our giant pile near the front door.

"Speaking of your sister—when do we have to leave to pick her up?" she shouts from the other side of the apartment.

"All taken care of," I say as I smile to myself.

"What?"

47

KENDALL

Still practically asleep, I throw on a pair of leggings and a light jacket. I quickly run a brush through my hair and put on some mascara to make myself look a little more presentable to meet my future sister-in-law. At least it feels like we're meeting for the first time.

Between the shock of last night and the exhaustion of being awake at this ungodly hour, I have not yet processed the fact that my present life is drastically altered from the version that I thought was my reality. As I glance around the condo, lit only by the faint light of a rising sun, the wind catches the white bedroom curtains and this visual instantly triggers a memory—

I am driving in my brother's old beat up Camry across an expansive stretch of desert. The wind whips through the car, and beads of sweat form on my forehead and neck and evaporate into the dry oven of a car. My stuff is packed into the back of the small interior and Mike is asleep, his head resting on the passenger door, and his white undershirt billowing out with the passing air. The rising sun casts long amber colored bands of light over everything, and I have to squint into it to see the long, flat road before us.

I never understood the overwhelming size of the world until now—we've been driving for days and have not even left the country. Mike stirs, and taking off his sunglasses, rubs his eyes with his palms and lets out a typical Mike-groan.

"How much longer til Arizona?" he says, stretching his arms up into the car ceiling.

"Last sign said 140 miles," I say, mimicking his stretching and rolling my shoulders up and back to loosen up my tired body.

After driving for most of the morning, we switch at our lunchtime pit stop in the middle of nowhere. We share a pre-made peanut butter and jelly sandwich that tastes more incredible than any meal I've ever had, and Mike jokes about our crazy parents and their decision to sell the house.

"What the hell do they like about cruises anyway? If I wanted to spend the week fighting with fat Americans at a buffet I would just hang out at a Golden Corral."

I laugh, "Yea I don't get it either. I guess it makes them feel a part of something."

"Like diabetes?" Mike asks, holding out his soda towards me.

I take the cup and sip the sweet, bubbly liquid, laughing again at my brother and feeling content to just sit here all day.

"Okay let's get this over with," he says—the first thing I've disagreed with him on so far today.

Mike drives the rest of the afternoon and evening, and as the sun starts setting, we drive through Joshua Tree, stopping at Arch Rock and standing in awe at the massiveness of the rock formations. As we continue through the park, the rocks evolve into the familiar Joshua Trees of the Mojave Desert and I watch them drift by the car like phantoms that speak a secret language to my soul.

We stop at a motel just outside the west side of the park and crash, continuing our journey to my new life in Santa Cruz.

I remember now.

I just couldn't stay in Manhattan. It was so interesting and exciting and alive, but it was killing me. It's not fair to blame the city though because I thought it would give me an identity that I later discovered I had to create for myself.

So armed with my laptop and an idea, I wrote myself a manifesto of sorts, and got accepted into a writing program at UC Santa Cruz.

My idea was a manual for self-discovery. And my brother, who was also looking for the same thing, offered to drive cross-country with me to help us both find it.

As the memory fades out of my consciousness, I continue through my necessary tasks, paying the cab driver and making my way through security through a series of predictable steps. As I grab my backpack off of the conveyor belt and put my jacket back on, I walk towards the gates and the reality of all of this change finally hits me. I freeze in place and just begin to cry. I am now standing in the middle of the San Francisco airport sobbing hysterically. Rubbing my eyes and breathing deeply, I try to calm myself to no avail. I am now so hysterical that I'm legitimately worried that someone may call TSA on me.

Unstable woman with unmarked bag near security gate, I can hear them saying over the loudspeaker.

Since I'm over an hour early for my flight, I have the luxury of continuing my full-fledged breakdown in the privacy of the public bathroom. I run down the moving walkway, jumping off at the end and sprinting towards the ladies' room. I immediately head towards a stall and promptly throw up.

After rinsing my mouth out about a hundred times and buying some gum and coffee at the kiosk, I sit against the window and wait for my plane to board. As each minute creeps by, I feel the panic start to well up in my throat again. But something in my mind shifts without a huge amount of effort—I close my eyes and suddenly I'm back in the clearing in the woods lying on the cool grass. There are very few certainties in my life at this moment, but one that I cannot deny is that I have no control over my life. And in the dim light of dusk that night, in letting go of that urge for control, I finally remembered who I was.

I open my eyes and more people have gathered in the seats surrounding the gate. I sit and watch them, young and old, short and tall, just existing. Waiting to bump into each other. Or not.

I pull my phone out of my bag to check the time and a photo of my family smiles back at me from the wallpaper. I unlock the screen and decide to pull up the photos. The first is me, smiling at a table of some kind. I don't recognize my hair or outfit at first, but then, almost like remembering the pieces of a dream, I remember we were celebrating a milestone of some kind. The next is my mom and me, her hand over mine on the table. The next is of my brother drinking a beer and my dad looking disapprovingly at him from across the room. It was my NYU graduation dinner. This time, unlike the first, they were all there. I keep scrolling and scrolling and there are hundreds of candid shots of my family and friends, over and over and over again. My eyes well up with tears again, but these tears are different. They are tears of...relief.

—

After going through every photo in my phone twice, I am able to pull myself together again with more deep breathing and visualization. And I am also able to recall parts of myself that have evolved from the first version I had grown so accustomed to. I am a writer, a daughter, a sister, and a good friend. I am honest and unapologetic about who I am. I am free.

My phone rings loudly, startling me. The screen shines *Mandy* and the name is not immediately familiar but I answer it anyway, "Hello?"

"Kendall. Good news."

"Mandy?"

"Yea?"

"How do I know you?"

Mandy is silent for a beat, and then continues, "Cute. I need you do be serious for a second. We've had a breakthrough."

"Breakthrough?"

"With your book. Are you sitting down?"

"Book?"

"Newly-optioned book to be exact. IFC Films made us an incredible offer."

"No way."

"I'm your agent, would I lie to you?"

I pause, absorbing the words 'agent' and 'optioned' as if they are a foreign language that I learned years ago but had forgotten until now, "Mandy, can I ask you a question?"

"Sure, anything."

"What's this book about?"

"Um—okay. I'm not sure if this is a test or something, but it's about finding your truest self."

"Is it fiction or non-fiction?"

"It's a memoir."

I am so distracted with so many new memories that I even miss the first call for boarding, and by the time I'm on the tarmac the crew is already shutting all of the overhead bins. A few weeks ago, I would have ensured I had priority boarding and an aisle seat so I could silently judge everyone as they boarded the plane after me. Now, I am sure I look like hell, having cried my eyes out about fifteen times in the last twenty-four hours, and I almost missed my flight. But I feel a sense of camaraderie in the awkward smile of the young woman sitting next to me as I excuse myself and slide past her. I am also grateful when the pilot dims the lights in the cabin. I hide in my dark window seat watching the lights on the land below drift in and out of my vantage point.

After about two hours, my eyes are heavy but I can't look away, because the sun is rising, casting shadows over the snow-capped Rockies, and it is one of the most beautiful things I've ever seen. My heart feels heavy as I remember the time I spent falling down a mountain with the boy who's missing from my photos. I wonder where he is and if he and Courtney are still together. I wonder if he ever thinks about that kiss. He has no idea that it changed my life completely.

—

After the plane lands, and everyone on board texts or calls their loved ones from the runway, we all file out of the tiny pile of metal half-asleep and into the monstrous Denver terminal, full of glass, metal and monitors. I adjust the straps on my overstuffed backpack and throw my purse over my shoulder. There are people everywhere and the signs to ground transport lead to an escalator that feels like its two stories tall. I ride the moving stairs down, looking up at the giant paper airplanes that hang from the ceiling as some kind of art display. When I look back down towards the ground floor, there are a pair of familiar brown eyes looking back at me. My breath catches and I don't know what to do. Gavin is standing with a big duffel bag between his feet, wearing his old ratty hat backwards on his beautiful chestnut brown head. He stands with his weight on one leg and his arms crossed, his face impossible to read. His eyes follow mine, as I slowly exit the escalator and approach him. I stand a few feet in front of him and look down at his bag to hide my nervousness.

"Are you waiting for someone?" I ask, motioning towards his bag.

He looks me in the eye with an intensity that brings back a familiar ache deep in my core, "You," he says matter-of-factly, "Mike didn't tell you?"

I shake my head and look around, "Is Courtney with you?"

"Nope," he says and his big Gavin grin grows across his entire face. It's infectious and I can't help but smile back at him, "That might have been a little awkward considering we've been broken up for like five years."

He steps forward and picks me up easily, backpack and all, giving me a giant bear hug and swinging me around in a circle. I think I hold my breath the whole time because when he puts me back down I'm dizzy.

"C'mon we've gotta make a stop before we go see the happy couple," he says, taking my backpack off of me and putting it over his shoulder.

As we move along the highway that goes from Denver to Boulder, we make small-talk about our lives. I stick to the parts that I am certain about—my parents sold their house and moved into an oceanfront condo and apparently I stay there sometimes when they are busy cruising around the Caribbean. I am a writer and I am close with Mike.

"I still can't believe Mike's getting married," Gavin adds.

"Really? Why do you say that?"

"I mean, you know him best. He's always sworn he never believed in marriage."

"Oh, yea," I say, feigning agreement with something I'm not sure to be true.

"I think he just thought all girls were like Celeste," he laughs.

I chuckle at the idea and watch the trees fly by the truck window, thinking about how Celeste went from important to insignificant in my life in a matter of days, "I don't know, I think we all can be the worst version of our selves."

"I know," he looks over and smiles at me, "I mean, I know you think that. I read your book."

I am speechless and I just stare back at him in disbelief.

Finally, after staring at him for several minutes, and rubbing the goose bumps from my legs, I ask the question that has been brimming inside me, "And what did you think?"

"Twelve-ninety-nine is a bargain."

"What?"

"The price."

"I don't understand."

And Gavin just looks at me like he did all those years/days ago in the darkened hallway, his eyes shining with some look that I don't recognize, but that I can't look away from.

As we pull into a familiar apartment complex and Gavin cuts the engine, "I gotta get the last of the stuff I left here."

I follow him into the dingy old apartment where I was less than a week ago, but it's now almost entirely empty, save for the crappy old couch with familiar cushions. I stand awkwardly in the middle of the living room looking around at the worn wood paneling and hugging my arms to stay warm. Gavin comes back out from his old room with a small crate full of stuff. He puts it on the kitchen counter. He rummages through the box quickly and smiles. Looking over at me, his eyes meet mine.

"Ah-ha. I knew I saved it."

I walk over to the kitchen and he hands me a faded, beat-up piece of cardboard. On it are the words scribbled in my handwriting—

CITY-WIDE BLACKOUT TONIGHT
9:45 PM

I look from the cardboard back up to him and I don't really know what to say.

"Looks like you made it back alright," he laughs still looking at me, "Or have you not gotten in the elevator yet?"

"How do you remember that?" I ask, clutching the cardboard against my chest to hide my shaking hands.

He doesn't respond, he just steps towards me so that he is within inches of my face. I try to stand still and hope that this thin layer of cardboard keeps him from hearing my heart thumping loudly through my chest. He looks into my eyes like he's desperate to say something but nothing comes out of his mouth. He simply backs away, lowers his head and picks up the box, walking back towards the door. He stands in the open doorway and holds the door open for me to walk ahead of him. I don't move an inch.

"Where are you going?" I ask, frustrated.

"What are you talking about Kendall? We're going to see Mike and Jesse," his voice sounds terse.

"No. I don't want to go see Mike and Jesse yet."

"Okay—do you want breakfast or something? There's nothing here but we can stop and g—"

"No. I don't want breakfast."

"I'm so confused," he says, dropping the box on the floor in front of him and exhaling, "what do you want then?"

I can't hold back anymore so I don't. I cross the room instantly and put my hands on either side of his torso, look up in his beautiful brown eyes and kiss him desperately. I press my body against his and he lifts me to him, deepening the intensity of the kiss even further. His hands gently but firmly grasp the back of my head, holding me there, and I am hopelessly lost in the moment, right here, in the open doorway. And it is not perfect but it is incredible.

We kiss until Gavin gently touches my cheek and pulls back to look into my eyes, "Finally," is all he says, with a smile.

We both laugh as he picks me up and throws me onto the old couch, kissing me deeply and lowering his body onto mine until my mind is empty of anything except him. He takes my shirt off, and then his own and I run my fingers over the tattoo on his rib cage that I teased him about. But this time I am serious when I whisper, "Tell me what it means."

His copper eyes pierce straight through me, making my whole body cry out with a yearning I have never felt before.

"*Tiada yang tak mungkin.* It's Indonesian. It means, 'nothing is impossible'," and he kisses me again.

I giggle as I pull away from him, "Except traveling back in time and deciding not to get that ridiculous tattoo," I laugh so hard that my head falls in the couch next to his shoulder in laughter.

He grabs my hips and squeezes my torso just above them, tickling me and sending me back onto him as I erupt in more laughter.

After I catch my breath, I lean up onto my elbow and look into his brown eyes one more time.

"I'm sorry it took me so long," I say, tracing his jaw with my finger.

"Apology not accepted," he grins and pulls me against him, kissing me feverishly until I forget about everything.

48
EPILOGUE

GAVIN

I never really pressed Kendall for the details of what happened to her the night of the blackout. Mike has his theories, and I have mine. Despite the fact that I've loved her since I was seventeen years old, in doing so; I do believe that I've loved several people at once. It's hard to explain without making her sound completely insane, which she is sometimes, but I guess you would never understand unless you've known someone their whole life. Who also happens to be female.

"Kara! Stop!"

Her tiny hands press against the glass of the revolving door, resting there lightly as she freezes in place and looks back at me with her mother's beautiful green eyes. She grins and I put my hands above hers and we press the door forward together, stepping on each other's feet and laughing as we slowly rotate towards the lobby.

"Daddy! We're gonna get stuck!" she giggles.

The door opens to the interior and she runs immediately to the familiar group that's waiting by the elevators.

"Aunt Jesse!" Kara yells as she hugs her around her legs and looks back at me, "Daddy, where's Mommy?"

I smile, preparing my typical response—

"Mommy's taking the stairs.

Made in the USA
Middletown, DE
29 August 2018